Fish Drink Like Us

Pretend Genius Press

London, New York, San Francisco, Seattle, Washington D.C.

www.pretendgenius.com

Published simultaneously in the United States and Great Britain in 2006
by Pretend Genius Press
London, New York, San Francisco, Seattle, Washington D.C.

This compilation copyright © Pretend Genius Press 2006
Edited by Feargal Mooney

ISBN 0-9778526-1-X

Contents

i

Contents

Contents

Introduction

In the beginning were four drunken editors and their girlfriend/wives in a Midtown Manhattan bar. Four drunken editors et al whose recollections would equal at least eight or sixty four different genesises - or is that genesi? They might have argued the proper plural if given the cue but their lines were cast for bigger fish. They shared a philosophy that was species neutral. An empty hook will snag a catch eventually. And what have you caught?

"Well, this looks like some kind of Perch, which reminds me of Canary. And that's the book industry. That's a cage you carry around until its prisoner is dead."

"My catch is longer, a slithier silver."

"Slithy earn."

"This fish is pretty fat, and in this sense not good, but it does have whiskers and what's more this fish brags."

"It's too bad the hook gashed up one side of this guppy because if you could excise that whole side, the rest..."

"Tasty... Shrimp."

"A tiny penis fish."

And undoubtedly time went by when no fish were snagged. That's when you turn to talk to the bartender or excuse yourself to where the most genisi are found, which is at the urinal. One should piss fish as well as catch them because that's exactly the kind of fish we're looking for. Well, as it turns out, that is to say in the end, it's not the fish you hook but the accidental fish that slaps your ankle. It swims by and you never even really see it. It reads its way accidentally into your boat.

Bloog Mandrake

NY NY USA

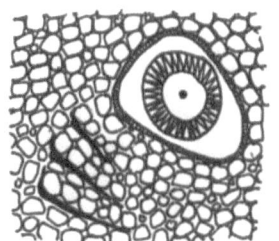

Jeremy BeBeau

Stigmatic Strippers and Erotic Endgames

MEREDITH IS DOWNSTAIRS, watching an over-muscular black man having his g-string taken off by an overweight bride-to-be. The woman is having difficulty; Meredith wonders if the woman's behavior will betray the color of her wedding gown.

For a moment she considers—as she does every week at some point—going back upstairs to watch Bill watch the women, but he has made her promise. A half an hour: alone time. She looks down at her watch—10:05. She left him upstairs only five minutes ago. She's not jealous or worried; but she does [she thinks] love him more than he loves her. So she'd waited for the least attractive girl to begin dancing before she slowly descended the red carpet stairs.

††† †

BILL IS UPSTAIRS, having a dollar bill taken out of his mouth by a large set of surgically enhanced tits. He hears the girl thank him as he finishes off another bottle of High Life. He looks down at the watch Meredith bought him. It's already been five minutes? Bill whistles. A pair of legs appears. "Another one," he says, motioning to his empty bottle.

A couple minutes later he is nearly finished. The breasts bounce back into his field of vision, nipples the size of shot glasses searing his retinas. He smiles, holds out another dollar. This time the girl pulls her g-string away from her hip and allows Bill to slide the money in between. "Thanks, Bill," she whispers.

He and Meredith have been coming here every Wednesday since September. Bill sighs, takes another drink of his beer, and looks down at the watch: 10:07.

~ ~ ~

MEREDITH LOOKS DOWN AT HER WATCH AND TAKES A DRINK. He's still got twenty-three minutes. The woman is attacking Nantucket Nate's g-string.

Meredith takes another sip of her gin and tonic and looks closer: every time the woman succeeds in pulling the elastic band of Nate's g-string down an inch or two, he slyly spreads his legs (thereby increasing the distance from the outer edge of one thigh to the outer edge of the other) and the red, silky band of his underwear slides back into its original position. The bride-to-be seems to realize [thinks Meredith] that her success wouldn't be quite as much fun. Her fiancé must be a special case. Meredith wants to ask her how they've done it.

Some of the women—women for whom passion has a finish line—await the unveiling anxiously, and one of the more aggravated spits, "For Chrissake, Barb, tear that fucking thing off!"

† † †

"TAKE IT OFF!" yells a man to Bill's left. The girl removes her denim vest and places her cowboy hat on Bill's head. "You like the Wild West, Bill?" she whispers. He smiles slightly and hands her a dollar.

That's where Meredith wants to go. Wants both of them to go. Bill stands up and moves to a small round table a little farther from the stage.

A young man has been holding up a dollar bill for some time. He looks nervous, somewhat agitated. It might be the first time [Bill thinks] he sees an unrelated, three-dimensional naked woman. The young man reaches deep into the pocket of his drooping khaki pants and pulls out a five-dollar bill. He still seems ignored. "What, my money's not good enough?" he says, loudly enough for everyone to hear. "Is my money not good enough?"

~ ~ ~

SHE'S HAD ENOUGH, Meredith thinks. Barb had worked Nate's g-string down below his knees; she continued pulling down, down past his calves, down past his ankles—down until her chin hit the stage's mirrored floor.

"Shit," exhales the woman who'd been most adamant earlier. Her less than enthusiastic reaction confirms what Meredith had already guessed: she, at least, had never been here before.

Barb looks into the floor, looks at the reflection of Nate's shoed foot. She follows it up, up past his ankles, up past his calves, up past his knees and finally to the g-string that Nate wears underneath the first to facilitate legal audience participation.

"Again?" Barb asks, raising her chin from the floor as Nate shakes his head and offers her a hand. The soft red glow of neon illuminates her teeth and shines off of her hair as she shrugs and fingers her engagement ring.

Meredith turns away from Barb, takes a drink, and focuses on her watch—10:15.

† † †

BILL WALKS UP TO THE BAR, orders a High Life, and looks down at his watch: 10:15. "Here you go," says the bartender, removing the cap and handing him the bottle. "Enjoying yourself?"

Bill shrugs.

"Your woman."

Bill shrugs again and takes a drink of his beer.

"There's a cure," Ken offers, his eyes motioning to a few girls along the opposite wall. Bill recognizes the breasts.

"They haven't cured me yet." Bill says. After the first two weeks Wednesday night sex—if it is had at all—differs only in distance: now it is her. It isn't working for either of us [he thinks] glancing again at the girls.

"They could, Bill."

Tiffany meets his eyes and blows him a kiss. He catches it in the air and puts it in his pocket. Valerie turns her back to him and bends down to grab her spurs. "Wanna go West?" she mouths, upside down and backside up.

Meredith had asked him the same thing many times. But he'd never felt like saying yes then. He did now.

She'd dump me, he thinks; she'd definitely dump me. "They could," he says, raising his bottle and making his way towards the bathroom. He reaches in his pocket, purses his lips, and closes his eyes.

"They could."

~ ~ ~

"YOU LADIES DEFINITELY DON'T WANT TO GO ANYWHERE!" The announcer yells, quite aware of the anticlimax moments before. "Get up, get yourself a drink, and get ready. Because in five minutes Kid Cock is going to rock!"

Meredith watches Barb and the angry woman gather their things and lead the rest of the women up the stairs side by side. She will get herself a drink, she thinks. After she goes to the bathroom.

Meredith stands up and looks around the room. Completely empty, now; except for a woman in the opposite corner. Meredith sets down her nearly empty glass and walks slowly towards the bathroom, nodding at the bartender on the way. He smiles, nods back, and motions to the woman in the corner, silently saying, "Check it out." Meredith does. The woman is stationary. She turns back, unimpressed. "Look at her hands," the bartender mouths.

Meredith's eyes follow the woman's arm underneath the table. A necklace? She looks up at Stanley, then back to the woman's face: eyes closed, head bowed, lips moving fervently.
"Crazy," she says aloud, pushing the bathroom door open.

✝ ✝ ✝

IT'S CRAZY, Bill thinks, pushing the bathroom door open. But it just might work. He checks the stalls, and, after finding them all empty, enters the one nearest the wall. He covers the toilet seat with a few layers of toilet paper and finds himself scanning the walls for graffiti. There are the normal obscenities and phone numbers, gay bashers and Christians—1 COR 11.9 is etched into the blue paint—but one in particular catches Bill's eye. "Shit or get off of the pot," he reads.

~ ~ ~

POT, she thinks. She wants to giggle at what isn't funny and/or become, if only momentarily, emotionally apathetic. She places both of her palms flush against the mirror, framing the reflection of her face.

"He doesn't love me," she states as matter-of-factly as possible, before breaking down: "But why?"

She watches her lips remain stubbornly silent and tears tremble at her eyelids.

"Only one can…" a constipated voice seems to answer.

Meredith scans the mirror. Empty. She turns and looks around the room. A fluorescent light flickers. A pair of feet in the nearest stall. "Are you, are you talking to me?"

"Accept it," says the breathless voice.

Meredith crouched down.

"Coming…" A grunt.

"Excuse me—"

"…out!"

Meredith leaps up and pushes through the bathroom door. It closes behind her. In the bathroom a toilet flushes. The table where the crazy woman was sitting is empty; the necklace remains. "Another of the same?" the bartender asks as she approaches.

Meredith nods in confirmation as she checks the time—10:19.

† † †

ELEVEN MINUTES. Bill washes his hands and checks his breath. High Life, he thinks. My Life.

~ ~ ~

HER DRINK SEEMS STRONGER, the room seems darker. The music that started as Nate left the stage has stopped.

"Ladies," says a voice. Meredith looks around. Don't you mean lady? she thinks. "Ladies, are you ready?" Meredith doesn't answer. "I said, are you ready?"

"Yes, I am ready," answers Meredith.

"Are you ready for Kid Cock?"

"Yes, I am ready for Kid Cock," she intones sarcastically.

The lights turn off; the music starts quietly:

"Bawitaba da bang a dang diggy…"

Her pulse rises with the volume.

"…up jump da boogie…"

A spotlight—

† † †

"A HIGH LIFE," says Bill, answering the silent inquiry of the bartender as he walks away from the bathroom door. Tiffany is slightly closer now; she seems to be working her way down the bar. Slowly. "Actually, Ken," he says quickly, "give me a kamikaze, instead."

Ken follows Bill's gaze and smiles, "Bill, my boy, this drink's on me!"

Tiffany laughs. He watches her raise her left hand to her blond locks. He can tell her armpit is smooth. If she doesn't make it to my end of the bar before 10:30 [he thinks] I'm going to her. Meredith will see us. And when she does—

"I know plenty of veterans who'd sleep better if kamikazes kept that still," Ken says. "Drink up!"

Bill raises the glass to his lips and throws his head back. When his vision clears he looks at his watch: 10:20.

~ ~ ~

MEREDITH HAS STOPPED CARING WHAT TIME IT IS. The moment the light came on she understood.

He stood, arms perpendicular to his body, legs crossed at his ankles, chin resting against his bare chest. Long, brown, stringy hair fell over his face. A large crucifix hung around his neck, and a 40oz bottle of malt liquor was in his right hand. He wore red wristbands on each of his wrists.

Sacrifice, Meredith thinks, closing her eyes. But would Bill give something up?

She opens her eyes. Another one can. Kid Cock slides to the front of the stage; for a moment the mirrored floor makes it look like he is walking on water. Meredith takes a drink, rises from her seat, and walks towards the stage.

"Thanks, Kid," she says, dropping a five dollar bill. "Goodnight."

"Thank you," he replies, "but please, don't leave. I hate to dance for no one."

"I've seen what I needed to see."

"But I haven't even taken off my pants yet," he says.

"You didn't have to," Meredith says, turning towards the stairs.

† † †

TWO MORE MINUTES. And then he'll go to her. Tiffany is caught up in a conversation, and time is running out. Bill looks at his watch: 10:25.

"Another shot, Ken," Bill says.

"You got it, Bill. But you'll have to pay for this one."

"I have no problem with that."

Ken walks the length of the bar and, on his way back, stops and whispers something to Tiffany.

"Enjoy."

"Thanks," Bill says, taking the shot. He sets the glass down a little too loudly, and looks over at Tiffany. She looks up, smiles, and starts to walk towards him. Here we go, Bill thinks. She can do it.

Her high-heels bring Tiffany slowly nearer, her bright lips part to reveal her bright teeth. He wills himself erect. The decision will be made for him. He begins fabricating and rehearsing lines silently:
I'm sorry, Meredith. Please, forgive me. I'll try not to do it again.

It's only been going on for two or three months.

She only ties me down when I ask her to.

Bill likes the sound of that one.

The young man who was so aggravated earlier steps between Bill and Tiffany. Bill clenches his right fist and looks at his watch. No time. He takes one step forward and stops.

The boy has one hand on Tiffany's ass and one in his pocket. He extends himself, stands on his toes, and whispers something into her ear. She looks down at him, seemingly waiting for something else. He brings his hand out of his pocket and shoves something between her breasts. Tiffany looks down for a moment, looks over at Ken, turns away from Bill, and escorts the boy out the door.

Bill hears Ken yell after her: "Be back in twenty minutes, Tiff!"

Bill quickly checks his watch: 10:28. "High Life, Ken. Now. Please." Ken quickly brings him his beer.

"You know, Bill, she'll be back—"

He turns away angrily. What was he thinking? He hurries over to the table where Meredith had left him and attempts to regain his composure. She'll be up here any minute. She's good; I'm lucky.

Bill takes a drink of his beer and checks his watch: 10:29. One minute. Thirsty. Another drink. Content.

10:30—where is she? We synchronized just before she went downstairs. Bill feels weak but stands up.

Stay with me Meredith. Don't leave me alone, Meredith.

He runs through the room, down the red carpet stairs, and stops on the threshold of the quiet room. He looks in; and sees no women. The bartender is emptying ashtrays. The stripper has a rosary in his hands.

Barry Blumenfeld

In San Felipe

For days now, Blanche had been expecting something to happen. She went about things as usual, going to work at the Valhalla Drinx where she was a hat-check girl, eating lunch at the truck-stop next door, picking through the magazine racks afterward, looking for something, looking for something. It was hot in San Felipe. Southern California in August: the air shimmers, palm trees wave through the shimmering. She liked to wear white tennies, but heat of the pavement came through the rubber soles. It was always nice to get back to the Valhalla, into the dark cool of the air-conditioning. In there it was always midnight. The rumbling air-conditioner, the hiss of the bar hose tap spouting bubbly water, the cool flamenco guitar music they piped in over the Muzak. She had to work in a booth next to the door, patrons opening it to let the sun glare in. She could feel the gust of dry heat. She was new, so she worked the day shift. No tips. But the last few days, every time that door opened, Blanche looked.

The person silhouetted against the light might be the one. The one what? She wasn't sure. It wasn't too clear. She was simply waiting.

When the light outside was finally going, at nine, Blanche's shift would be over. She had a bicycle she liked to ride home on. She liked cutting through the breeze as the temperatures cooled and the white-blue daylight shaded little by little into violet and the sun going down made gold and purple strips over the ocean, sometimes on the clouds too, when there were clouds, bottoms painted like golden cotton candy, royal shadows on the wispy fringes. It was warm compared to the inside of the Valhalla, and the smell of the sea came in on the breezes. Blanche loved the ocean, it was just over the horizon. The desert around San Felipe came right up to the water. In the sky sometimes the vultures circled, but every evening around dusk there were seabirds in ravenous screaming hordes.

The same ride every night: along the neon strip back into town, trucks booming by to her left as she pedaled down the straight level road between the highway and the drainage ditch. Straight ahead into that sunset, straight towards the Pacific. Sometimes she thought of keeping on. Right through town, right past her apartment court, over the scrub and the sand. The sand wouldn't bog her down, she'd fly right over it, her wheels would be skimming and singing. Right over the glassy wet sand the last thing before the ocean, then beyond. Magic bike. The ocean curved away and where it fell below the horizon, that was Hawaii, that was China and Tahiti. The men in nothing but sarongs, women with beautiful blue orchids in their hair. The cool sweet ocean breezes.

The apartment was small, but Blanche made it pretty. There was light everywhere, yellow sheer curtains, bright potted flowering plants. She had geraniums in a window box, Degas prints on the walls. This time of year there was a lot of daylight left, even after her shift. She put a tape on, Al Dimeola, and stepped into the shower. The grit of the road washed away, the hot water brought a flush out on her breasts. Then she lay down naked on the bed, without the air-conditioner. The heat dried her. The sheets were smooth, comforting. She would sleep and the same dream would come. A waterfall: cool boulders behind her, the falls concealing her from the woods beyond. Violets in the grass, intense. She was singing the most haunting, the most beautiful song. A man was singing too. She was singing with him. His voice moved her beyond anything in her real life. It was knowing, sad and kind, she wanted to melt into it. There was a place she once had been. She wanted to go back there, but the song said it was lost, forever lost. Always the same thing then: a growl, deep-chested, huge. A panther would emerge from the white effulgence and penetrate the sheets of water with its yellow eyes. A panther, huge, muscles under a coat of bright black fur. Belly brushing the grass, coming close. The sunlight around it, blinding, blinding. It thrust its head into the curtain of water. The crashing stream would soak its face, its fine coat would separate into little clumps like the tips of paint-brushes. It would open its jaws: the tongue and the gums so pink, glistening. Its breath so heady and intense, vomitous acid reeking of stomach juices and saliva.

Blanche would wake with that smell in her nostrils, heart skittering. Wet, down there.

A man at the bar was watching her. She felt him nearly every night, out in the darkness. Sometimes, she thought she heard his voice, hearing him talk to a woman on the stool to his left. Blanche felt that he always took the second bar stool from the extreme left, the end of the bar nearest her. Only a few feet separated the hat-check booth and the cash register from that side of the bar, but she couldn't see the man because there was a pool of yellow light between them, pouring in from the billiards room that gave onto the dining-room there. He was protected from her gaze. Blanche imagined him as small, bony, a big Adam's apple bobbing under the skin of his throat. A black-haired man in a flowered shirt. A gold tooth. Not handsome. She tried not to think about him, but he seemed to be in there nearly every day, invisible, watching her from the darkness. She wasn't afraid, not really. Men were always staring at her, she was still young. And besides, it was daytime, at least it was outside. Just beyond the leatherette door with its rusty shiny studs and its little square window. The strip bathed in glare: cacti, trucks, cars.

"Thank you." As she handed the man his jacket the voice muttered it, the same one she had to strain to hear through the flamenco music and the ice tinking and the air-conditioning. She was sure. It was clear. He wasn't small; he wasn't ugly. A blond man in his thirties. He was wearing the flowered shirt, though, the same one she had imagined. His forehead was tanned and flaking, a little leathery, pinkish swatches of skin underneath. Thick hair, highlights in the incandescent light from the bar. He stared as she handed him the jacket. Pale blue eyes. Then out the studded door. He disappeared into the glare. He was a black smear in the center of that white power, shrinking, melting.

It was four-thirty and Blanche had only just come back on, but she opened the waist-high gate to the hat-check booth and whispered "Right back" to the cashier and followed the blond man into the street. She looked to the left and the right, the sidewalks were empty. Trucks, heat, vultures. The smog from Los Angeles was a violet dome to the north. She stood there, wondering what to do, wondering what she was doing. Then he pulled up from around back. It was a red Porsche. The headlights were covered with a black leather mask. Leaning over the death seat he said, "Come on." The red door swung open and Blanche got in. She could smell leather and oil.

He was smiling, one eyebrow perching higher than the other. Blanche wanted to say something, but there was nothing she could think of. She watched him as he pulled onto the strip, brown forearms on the wheel. He looked strong. Gold hair on the arms and poking between the buttons of his red, blue, green flowered shirt.

"I just want to drive for a while," she said.

"All right," the man answered, nodding.

Blanche relaxed in her seat, thinking it was crazy. The man turned a switch and the air-conditioning came on. She said, "No, turn it off. Please."

He did it. Blanche rolled the window down and the hot wind buffeted her.

The man said, "You are terrific. I've been looking at you for days."

"Let's not talk now," Blanche said.

"Sure," the man said.

They were headed for town. Blanche said, "Turn around, towards the desert."

"Sure," the man said again, and swung a U-ee with rubber squealing. The road was empty, his bravado was empty. She didn't like that. It was strange, she felt mean, she felt control.

"I want to fuck you in the desert," she said. He didn't answer. "And then I want to go to the beach. I want to do it by the ocean."

"Anything you want," the man said. He laughed. He hooted. He yelled, "Shit!," wagging his head.

The strip was behind them now. Ahead, the brown scrub and the empty sky.

After a while, Blanche said, "This is good. Stop here."

He cut the gas and let the red Porsche coast slowly to a halt. The car listed to its right. There was a grade from the blacktop and in its shadow a little gully.

"Do you think there are snakes down there?" Blanche said.

"No snakes hereabouts," the man said.

"You lie."

"No!"

"You want me in that dirt. You don't care about anything else. You don't give two shits about any snakes."

"You're a smart lady." He grinned. He had a pair of sunglasses on now, aviator style, gold rims. He looked stupid.

"I'm dreaming," Blanche said.

He leaned over and put a hand on the back of her neck. It was big, it sent a chill down her spine. She had goose bumps. He pulled her towards him and kissed her on the mouth. She smelled beer, pulled back.

They stared at each other.

The man said, "What?"

"What would you do if I changed my mind?"

He shrugged, smiling, eyes masked.

"Would you hurt me?"

He laughed, shook his head. "Jeez, a live one."

"Did you ever hurt a woman?"

He laughed again. "Jeez! Don't talk like that, lady, you're making me nervous."

"God. God. God." She rubbed her face, stroked her cheeks downward, then in circles.

"It's getting awful hot in here," the man said. "Do you want to do something or not?" He reached over, put his hand under Blanche's left breast. He lifted it. She felt a it go from the nipple straight down to her cunt: a thrill like electric current. She moaned and he put the hand inside her white cotton blouse, three fingers between the top two buttons, rough fingers, rubbing the skin there, scraping it.

She said, "Stop." The man had both hands on the buttons, he was too clumsy. Blanche said "Stop" but the man didn't, he was trying to undo the buttons. They wouldn't come. He said, "Shit!" His mouth was opening, the tongue was like a snail, it was like a penis, the beery breath.

"Stop," Blanche repeated, but she had her hands down on the seat, gripping the seat in her two fists.

"Christ!" the man said. He put both hands on the edges of her blouse, curled the thick fingers inside and yanked. The blouse came undone. He was leaning over her. He put his whole mouth on hers, his tongue was in there, thick like a thick python. She was gagging. She retched. He reared back, bumped his head on the low ceiling, grunted "Shit." Blanche had sour yellow vomit on her blouse. He tugged at it, pulled it out of the elastic band at the waist of her pink slacks.

"What are you doing?" Blanche said.

"Fuck you," the man said and slapped her, two strokes with the right hand.

She covered her face and said, "Don't be mad, please don't be mad."

"Shut up. I have a knife, bitch. You little bitch." He had her blouse off, he was putting the fingers into her bra, they were seeking the nipple. His left hand was on her right shoulder, holding her down. She pushed against it and he pushed her down into the seat. He was strong. Blanche stopped struggling. He was pulling at the elastic band of the slacks, tugging them over her hips. He got them down around her knees. Pink panties, wet at the center, she could feel it, his hand was right there. "Bitch," he said. "Bitch. Bitch." He was wriggling, left hand on her shoulder, right hand now catching his buckle, his zipper. He got it; he got it down. He was panting, smoker's wheeze. He put his hand back over her vulva, clutched it too hard.

"Please," she said.

"Take them off, you cunt." He was pulling his briefs down with both hands. She saw his buttocks rise, brown hair on the pale skin. She had an urge to laugh but she bit her lip instead, she cut it. Then she felt his hands on her knees. She tried to scream but her throat clenched air, the voice wouldn't form. She wanted to vomit again, then he pushed into her. He wasn't very big. He pushed hard, just once, and his back arched, he winced and groaned. He still had the sunglasses on. He sighed: long, thin, like a baby's squall. He said, "Wow." He pushed at her between the legs, pushed her into the seat, but it was limp, it was gone.

"Sorry 'bout that," he said.

Blanche was staring out the window with his weight on her. Her bare feet pointed out the windows, one each side. Ridiculous. She could see a vulture up there, dipping one wing then the other, coming down. Pale sky.

"You like the rough stuff," said the man.

"What do you mean?" Blanche was panting, rage coming up like tears.

"What now," he said, lifting up, elbows stiff, weight on his hands.

"You bastard."

"It'll be better next time." He grinned. "At the beach."

"No."

"Hey, I'm just warming up!" He caressed her under the chin. "I like you. Let's see a smile."

"You threatened me. You called me a cunt."

"I wouldn't hurt you, babe!" He patted the glove compartment. "That's just here for emergencies. I just got carried away, hon." He rolled off her. They struggled to upright positions as a caravan of sixteen-wheelers rolled by. Four, just above them. Blanche could see the shotgun riders in their cab windows. One looked at her, his eyes popped, then he was gone.

"I want it different at the beach," she said.

"Anything." He was sticking his underpants over his feet.

She sat there nude except for her bra, watching him dress. The Porsche was an oven, her behind slipped along the slick cushions on a layer of sweat.

"It's hot. Let's go," she said.

The man glanced at her. "Like that?"

"Let's drive over to the beach right now."

"Sure, honey." He did as she told him. Blanche was trying to think of something. They did another squealer on the highway. It was busier now. She thought: let them look.

The man said, "Can you believe it. Right through town. Holy Christ."

Blanche said, "I'm sure these things happen every day."

"They don't to me, babe." He was hitting the gas at every light.

"You'll get us killed," Blanche told him.

"You'll get us busted," the man answered.

They got through the town. It was seven or eight and the sun was low. It was settling in a wallow of its own fire. Clouds hung out there in immense bands, violet. Blanche felt that was the light of Heaven shining between them. Angels were there.

I am the light of the world.

She said, "I'm crazy, right? I have to be."

"You're a good kind of crazy, sweetheart, sweet honey. I'm going to make you happy up there." He nodded towards the beach in front of them. The road bent right, to the north. The man drove straight ahead, onto a rise next to the left lane. The Porsche coasted into a clump of tall reeds, stopped.

"This is better," Blanche said. It was. It was cool here. Gulls were calling. Terns with black-tipped beaks that hooked down swooped across the sand looking for food in the wire garbage cans. The sweet salt ocean breath, the glory shimmering on the rough surface of the water.

"I want this to be just like a dream," Blanche said.

"Uh huh." He had his glasses off, finally. She could see his eager, worried eyes.

"Put them on again," she said.

"It's getting pretty dark."

"Put them back. Please." He did it.

"I wish I could see you better."

"I'll show you everything." She opened the door on her side and stepped into the reeds. She unhooked her bra, gaily flung it away. She raised her arms, stretched herself towards the sky. She felt his eyes on her from the driver's seat, on her arms, her bare sides, her belly, her breasts.

"Come here and touch me," she said.

The man opened his door and Blanche said, "Wait." He stood there looking, door open, eyes masked. She was still on tiptoes stroking the empty air.

"Can you see?" she asked.

He nodded.

"What? Tell me."

He shrugged, shook his head, stuck his hands in his pockets. He said: "Shit!"

"Tell me I'm pretty," Blanche said. She put the tips of the fingers of her two hands together in a little arch and pirouetted.

The man went to take the glasses off and Blanche said, "Don't you do that."

"I wish I could see you. You're pretty, all right."

She could see his erection. He was in tan chinos. It made the front of them look like the prow of a ship.

"Am I driving you crazy?" she said.

"Yeah."

"Come here and touch me, just touch me." He walked towards her slowly and, when he was a few feet away, reached out with his left hand and touched her right breast.

"That's right," she sighed, "that's right," as his hand skimmed the surface of her belly and brushed the brown puff of hair below. The birds were still calling, she could hear that. His hand went deeper and Blanche said, "No," and the man pulled his hand out right away.

"Smell it," she said.

He sniffed his fingers.

"Do you like my smell?"

"I like your smell."

"What do I smell like?"

He licked his lips and then he said, "I don't know. Smells good."

"But what is it like."

"It just smells like a clean cunt."

He went to unbuckle his belt, but she said, "Wait."

The man put his hands down. The palms faced her. The hard-on stuck out, looking desperate.

"Does it hurt?" she asked.

"It aches."

"Do you believe this is real?"

"I hardly do."

"Take your clothes off now."

He dropped his pants. She saw his hard little penis reaching out for her out of a sparse cloud of yellow hair. His balls were retracted, two compact pink eggs.

The man stepped out of the chinos and Blanche said, "Stay there."

"Come on lady!"

"Do it there."

He stared at her with open mouth. His loose shirttails wafted in the breeze, blue and green and rosy-red. Then he sank to his knees groaning "Oh my God!" and clenched it in both fists, squeezing it. White gobs spurted, landed in the grass. She looked at the small purple head, white fluid on it, drool. Disgusting.

Something in Blanche relaxed, a weight sagged voluptuously. A hot something was flowing inside her, her breath came faster. She felt a soft breeze lifting perspiration off her, cool. She laughed, drew her hands together above her head and brought them down in a praying gesture. She leaned over, cackling, screeching, she could feel her neck and face going scarlet with it.

Blanche panted deeply until she was a little calmer. She said, "Come over here."

The man stood, brushed sand from his knees, approached her. He placed his hands on Blanche's hips. She kneeled. It was getting stiff again, she licked it off. She licked it all off. She sucked it, pulling away and licking her lips so they'd slide over it. The shaft was extraordinarily smooth, Blanche felt every silken ridge with her lips. There was a faint smell, too, of his balls. Roaring surf foaming on the sand behind him, reeds waving dark green in tufts. The sand was glassy, it reflected black specks, birds circling.

His pelvis began to thrust, the prick hitting the back of her throat was too much. Blanche gagged on him, she pushed him away. But then she wanted him again, wanted to suck all of it and swallow it. She reached behind and grasped his buttocks and pulled him towards her. His hands were on her shoulders. She mashed her face against him, her nose flattened to one side on the hard bone. The blond hair was on her lips and in her nostrils, coarse and fresh like shampoo. He did smell like shampoo, it was Herbal Essence! She sucked and she sucked, his prick swelled up in her mouth against the back of her throat. But the gagging was still too unpleasant, Blanche thought she might heave. She pulled back.

The man said, "Unbelievable."

She squatted slowly down, lower and lower until she could feel the strands of hair between her haunches brush the ground. The hair was long there, she liked that, it was her secret pride. She swayed, letting the brushing motion caress her.

"Come on," she said, sinking down, rolling onto her back. Grass and stones. She was wide open. He leaned over, cast his shadow on her. His small beer paunch touched her, the hair brushed the skin of her belly. He found her opening, the prick sank in. He was small, though, she didn't like it very much, she couldn't feel him.

Blanche said, "Do it harder." He began to ram it, he was grunting with the work of it. She twirled his hair around her fingers. It was beautiful, brassy hair shining in the red light of the setting sun.

"My God," the man said. He winced. His back arched, Blanche knew he was coming. She felt it pulse inside her.

"Oh no no no," she moaned. She yanked at his hair. "Don't stop. Keep going," she said.

"I can't." He collapsed. He was a dead weight all over her.

"Blanche moaned: "No. No."

The man stirred. "Sorry."

Her hips were circling under him. Her fingers held his hair. She said, "Do something." She was lifting her buttocks up so his weight would cause friction where she was sensitive. She rubbed against him. He tried to thrust, but it was lost. He pulled out. Blanche reached downward and gripped herself. She rubbed it. The man watched her. She closed her eyes, she didn't want to see him looking. She lifted herself and rubbed, nothing touching the ground between her heels and her shoulders. She was all in the air. Her fingers went inside rapidly thrusting. Her free hand on the left breast, touching the nipple. It happened finally, in rapid squeezing fluttering in there. It was like little guns going off, but it was only muscles. The swampy heat she had felt before was gone. She passed the scream over her voice box, not through it, she didn't want him to hear anything. All he heard was her panting.

Blanche opened her eyes. He was looking at her, she didn't want him to. The frames of his glasses were red-hot in the sunset.

"Get my clothes," she said.

He picked himself off the ground, brushing dirt off his knees and backside, went to the car, returned with her slacks and her blouse. Blanche dressed quickly. The man circled her neck with his left hand and kissed her mouth. She let him, she didn't kiss back. His tongue like a thick blind worm in there.

He backed off, walked away to look at the surf and the sun going down behind it. He still had nothing on. Blanche wished to say something, she couldn't find the words. She was upset. There was pain inside her that passed through her nose, the back of her throat, and ended as a sick feeling in the upper part of her stomach.

She came up behind him. The man had long hair around the nape of his neck, the hot breeze was whipping it. The metallic hair against the creased, sunburned neck was pretty. He sensed her there and turned, smiled.

"I'm going to take a nap," he said.

She followed him to the car. The Porsche was on a rise, aimed skyward. He lay down on the grass in front of the headlights, curled up on the crest of the rise. Blanch lay down next to him. The sun was half down. It was like a god of fire alone on all the waters.

When she woke, the stars were out. It was still very warm. The man slept next to her, knees up, like a fetus. He was still wearing sunglasses, no clothing. The engine was warm too, Blanche smelled the miasma of fuel.

She leaned against the black mask on the headlights of the Porsche. Waves were breaking on the sand in a slow rhythm. It was the breathing of a crystalline animal, an unbelievably enormous creature, something that surrounded her. It wasn't human, it wasn't even alive. She tried to think about it. She tried to imagine it breathing on the lone sea islands and the distant coasts of Asia.

She noticed the absence of the birds, listened for their sounds, but there was nothing. Only the empty road behind them, the Porsche, the man beside her, and the beach, the waves, the stars. Then she was dizzy. Her chest froze because the sky was so huge, so huge. It was as though it all turned up-side-down and she was floating on an ocean of stars with nothing between them and she might fall forward into the abyss between the stars. Blanche breathed rapidly, heavily. It was the only way to breathe at all. She screamed, the man groaned and shook his head.

Blanche stood up. She looked for the lights of San Felipe, the lights of a truck. Nothing. It was so dark. She felt along the side of the Porsche looking for the handle of the door. She found it and crawled inside. She felt along the panel for the lights. She turned on the light in the passenger compartment. Yellow light. She turned the headlights on, slid back out of the car.

The headlights were masked, but she could see the man by the light from inside the car. He was grey and she wanted to see colors. The color of his blue and green and rosy-red flowered shirt. Oh but he wasn't wearing the shirt. She went back into the front seat, found it, crawled out again, draped it across his back and shoulders. He trembled. She slumped next to him. The leather mask on the headlights was very hot on Blanche's neck, it burned. She stood up, fumbled with the mask, it was hot to the touch. She finally had it off. The headlights shone white, brilliant, their beams went off into outer space. The white light showed colors: his pretty hair, the exotic shirt. Blanche tossed the mask as far away as she could. That was not far, it twirled a few times and landed in the dust.

She sat next to the man. He slept deeply but once in a while he moved, he shifted a limb or he would mutter something she couldn't understand. She stayed next to him for hours.

She must have slept. The sky was a little blue in the east, just a faint pre-dawn blue instead of the black of night. Anywhere but directly behind the car, night was in full sway: stars and absolute blackness, no moon. Blanche sat up, her legs tingled. She went into the car. The lights were dimming, the battery was draining. But the headlights were still as white as anything shining into the west. Blanche opened the door to the glove compartment. There was the man's knife, it was a buck knife. It had a fancy bone handle, the blade was wide and short, the edge was hooked in the Oriental arc of a scimitar. She picked it up. It was light. She gripped it. Tight. Tight.

She stepped back out and sat next to the man. He was curled up facing her. His hands made two tiny fists near his face. The shirt lay on his back. His penis was little, pink, round in a nest of pubic hair.

Blanche brought the knife close to the prick's head, she scraped it lightly with the point. He didn't stir.

The sun was rising.

J. Tyler Blue

Charles Street Romance

I am tired of trying to be clever, I just want to tell you the damn story the way I remember it. It's about space and timing although some of you will think it is about a man and a woman. I guess it is about that too, but mostly it is about space and timing.

It doesn't start the way great stories start. It wasn't raining and I don't think it was that cold outside either. I didn't have my poncho or my umbrella. I just had me. I was wearing flip flops one size too large. Blue and worn, I don't think anybody ever noticed they were just a bit too big for me. My jeans were ripped near my heel from dragging on the ground and my shirt was beginning to fade from too many washings. I didn't think about meeting her that night but like I said, this story is about timing.

And space.

She wasn't that overly beautiful girl that you might be thinking about. Yeah, she was a blonde but sometimes it seems like all of them are these days. She had blue eyes and yeah, they were something to look at but you wouldn't stop breathing if she looked at you or anything. I liked the way she dressed, in jeans and some button up shirt of some sort that said "I'm from California" even though she was only from some town outside of Baltimore. For whatever reason it didn't seem fake on her, she wasn't trying to be what she was, she was just being it. You have no idea how attractive that was to me at that moment. How many times do we meet people who just slither around in their own skin trying so hard to project some fantasy image they have of themselves on to you. As if you care. As if you would give a damn that they really can't afford that watch or those shoes. I don't know maybe it's just me. Maybe it's because I wear flip flops from Wal-Mart that are one size too big.

So we started talking. How that came to be isn't so important. We started talking about politics and life and she had opinions. Not your everyday opinions like "I don't like Bush because the economy sucks" or "Republicans are liars." No, she had real reasons for her opinions, like something about the quality of the people Bush was selecting to be Justices and she rattled off some startling information about the problems of some of these candidates. It wasn't in that huffy puff way that some people do things. You know that way when people know something they get loud and excited and slam down the information upon your ears with triumphant arm waving. She did none of that and suddenly I became enchanted by the movement of her lips.

Nice and full formed they moved comfortably on her face. Sometimes I have noticed women speak quickly as if speaking were a crime or that their lips can only be perfect in the position they were in when the final bit of lip gloss was applied. She had such a beautiful slight smile that seduced me a good two feet away. What would they be like to bite? What if it was raining and I had an umbrella to protect her? I should have shaved.

Suddenly she had to go so I grabbed a napkin and wrote: "Kristin's fake number is:"

She smiled and stared at the napkin for a few moments. I think it was a new form of murder she was trying out. I said something like help but it came out as "Come on. A fake number, how hard could it be?"

She gave me a number.

Could this be some story I tell my children?

I called her and we went out. It wasn't a fake number and I wore real shoes.

I picked her up and she seemed a bit nervous but not overly.

"Have you been married?"

Yes, I said. More aware of how small my Civic is.

"Do you have kids?"

Yes, two. Wrong turn. Where am I going?

Don't look so upset I said. Please don't look upset I thought. Wouldn't a fake number feel better now? I wished it were snowing but it was too early for that.

Everything felt built up like a house of cards and as long as nobody touched it or no wind blows it might as well be a castle made of stone. We went out another night after that and then made plans for a Saturday. Then she said she couldn't see me. I said maybe some other time and she said sure. Some other time.

She called me later that same Saturday. She drove to a bar she had never been to. We kissed. She has beautiful lips. I played with her fingers between mine. We stood in silence and I didn't know who I was anymore. I called her. She was busy.

I called her. She was busy.

I called her. She was busy.

I never saw or heard from her again.

J. Tyler Blue

Fucking Alice

I got a gun. It ain't real but that don't matter. Nobody really know the difference anyways when I stick it up in they face. Like I did to this girl last night. All she did is scream. And yell and flop around and all this other crazy shit. She kept on saying her damn name to me like that would not make me want to fuck her. Or maybe she was trying to get me to fuck her. I ain't never fucked no Alice before. But really alls I wanted was some damn money.

See people like me we need what people like her got. Money. And nice shoes. And good clothes. And watches. Yeah, we need watches so we know what time these fools be getting off ov work so we can go rob they asses. I treat 'em like customers really. I say "Hey, welcome to my street. Now give me yur money bitch-ass!" And then I show 'em the gun. It's a damn good gun. Until Alice, that crazed bitch, broke that shit.

I went up to her all gentlemen like 'cause I know how these bitches are. All playa hatin' on anybody from the streets at first but after you gets to know 'em all they want is a little thug in 'em. So I goes up to her and say "Scuse me lady, you got a light?" Then I stood there all Clark Gable like but more modern, more P Diddy but a little more rugged. I had that smooth but hard look going. I had that shit down. I had it good cause as soon as I said it she damn near broke her leg trying to stop. She's all "Oh, I don't smoke." and all that shit but I wasn't gonna let this shit get away, you know what I'm sayin'?

So I start kicking my game and she was all eatin' it up like she was starving. She was straight up starving for some gangsta shit up in her. Man she was straight diggin' my shit. I was 'bout to just straight kick it with her, maybe go back to her place and hit it some but I had other shit to do that night. So I start walking her down this alley where I do my business you know. Not out where the po po can come and snatch me or some other damn fool and come try to be Superdude or whatever. I ain't no fighter. I ain't trying to get all up and sweaty and breakin' bones and that shit. Man I could prolly kill somebody if I throw a punch with all my might. I seriously hurt 'em. Damn fools, running up on me.

Anyway, I took her back in that alley, gave her my line. My line that I done put a paten on it. "Hey, welcome to my street. Now give me yur money bitch-ass!" It's all about delivery. It's all about timing and shit. Right when I say money that's when I break out the gun and I kind ov really give it to 'em on 'bitch-ass' for that added extra dimension ov effect. You know.

So I said that shit and she went up and started actin' a fool. Screaming her name "Oh I'm Alice, I'm Alice, Oh, Oh my god." And all that shit. Looking damn stupid. I was 'bout to shoot her ass but my gun didn't have any bullets in it. It was fake. So I just yelled at her. "Shut the fuck up Alice! Before I shoot yur ass!"

She did. Then I thought damn. I got mad game. I could probably make her suck my dick right now. She probably wanted to. The way she was eyeing me up and shit. She probably wanted to lick my asshole or some other kind ov freaky shit. Fucking freak. I was about to let her go right then because I was just like "Damn, why don't I just do what she wants me to do and then rob her ass." But then she just went off again. She looked like Jackie Chan but like a more bitch version ov it. All this monkey jumping and shit acting all crazed. I was like damn these rich girls got crazy ways ov wanting to sex people up! But she kicked the shit out ov my hand and broke my damn gun.

"My name is Alice!"

That scared the shit out ov me. Who the fuck got to be yellin' yur own name? I picked up the piece ov my gun and ran. I ain't scared to tell you that. This bitch is crazed. I ain't never fucking with no Alice again. Never.

Broke my damn gun. I really should ov punched her. But that ain't my style.

But damn.

Fucking Alice broke my damn gun.

Sean Brijbasi

Phonoplane

People want to be happy and control the future. There are no tyrants here. An approximate cross-pollination might suffice in this regard. Further. Was what was. Further.

Under the luau, the majus pristine, blanched by invisible particles and the timely life of my pedigree. Brrrrojo [restore] amarino [untie] azun [restore]. The difference between getting and the phonoplane. The difference between sleeping and the drier parts of stone. These things matter. You may find your way down the hill, after all.

At bottom a camel is human in so far as it is not spoken of first. We spoke of camels midstream and contemplated their bundle. An ancillary effect compensated for by our disdain for desert spittle.
The boy and his train. A faint bell stop unsummoned.

I knew it was all about him. This telling. To come so close to the understanding that he breathes finer air than I and not to breathe it. But who could take such a thing from him?

I carried his door-like plastic. Then he. And lay him on the blanket. Cornered west and straddled to find way of the girl (the girl). Frida. Whose hair covers his sleep. Who makes space in the morning for the sun to admire his face.

I want to tell you something about the boy Frida. Follow me to the meadow. And she did and the boy who came running out with sword and calling for me. Just to see. Those block-line filaments. The three [two] parts of sundry.

"It's time to go," she says.

But before I move we sit and look through the window. Maybe the frank (I think it plain). Maybe the dauphin: *in minor centuries.*

I am of the mind to leave her and let her find her own way.

"It's time to go," she says.

Like the time one made mention of greater things--first drop and penchant--I put him on his bicycle and sent him down the hill--unexpected ascension (a far point astray). I'll pick him up. I'll get him. Bring him from the station. Take a dance--and should an eyelid come undone--

Let me tell you about the boy Frida.

It's not easy to build a tree but I have gathered leaves for the pasting. Watch us from the balcony and feed on our gaze.

"I had a dream that normal friend-like budlings fell on my face and between them I saw the boy standing on a bare limb looking down on me."

Up there he seems smaller.

Connection [brings one greatness].

Connection [keeps one from becoming more].

An element of physiology. Stur. It will be all that is left when we are gone. The dream, sweetful and more famous than air, a thank you and good-bye. We may draw colors and swing free the hand and hammer but if the rain stops today and we sit shoulder to shoulder. She said my son. She said the camel. There are Romans here and the names of Romans.

Let me tell you Frida. I'll whisper so no one else can hear. Slowly.

The boy will love you.

X postulate. Chromosome decelerator. The phonoplane.

But then again, he may not.

Sean Brijbasi

The Last of the Undressed Children has Run By

a dark place of sadness and heartbreak

In Demerara palm trees exist. Clothiers tailor umbrellas. The hat brim of an old man looking down at his shoes gives one a feeling of inevitability. What once was, no longer is, and the drawings of giraffes and owls on the shower glass are washed away. Out there in the city the news girl stands in the middle of the road by a streetlight, fanning herself with the morning edition, shouting *young boy drowns in the river.*

Martin didn't want such things to be true but he knew they were true because life was like that. Things that shouldn't happen happen and if it weren't for a certain hardness in him, he believed he would collapse and die from pity. For he believed that pity--real pity--brought on a terminal condition. A dark place of sadness and heartbreak he was always trying to find a way out of.

He looked past the news girl's leg and saw half of the shop sign, which was enough to gather him up and place him at the door.

three and 1/fertile

Something woke him up.

The old man took off his hat and placed it near the crumpled newspaper on the space beside him. He pulled back his long, stringy hair and rubbed both eyebrows with the tips of his fingers. He wanted to be an army ranger and shoot people. Maybe save a little girl from being raped by guerillas and carry her to the safety of a helicopter. Old men had dreams too.

He leaned over and pulled off his right shoe and turned it upside down so that a small pebble fell out. He put the shoe on the chair. But he forgot to put his hat back on, so that when he hunched over to go back to sleep, his head dropped to the floor and rolled for three and a half miles before it stopped against the post of a broken-down, wooden fence that separated the road from the jungle.

tar-mata

The news girl opened the shop door. As she entered the small open space, the city came with her. The tops of buildings. Trees. The corrugated balconies and the clothes that hung over them. The glistening of traffic. The telephone wires. The noise. The clouds. The sun. They followed her wherever she went because they liked her. The news girl wasn't particularly fond of them so their fondness for her was mostly unrequited. She could do without the tops of buildings and the noise on most days. And she didn't have much use for balconies or the clothes hanging over them. The trees served her well on certain days when she didn't care much for the sun and the sun served her well on days when the clouds darkened her mood. She didn't think much about telephone wires. And the glistening of traffic bothered her eyes.

"What's for lunch?"

Sasha, who had been rubbing an apron against a wooden washboard, wiped the sweat from her forehead, and said: "drumsticks."

Martin sat at one of the tables near the window. Outside it became dark. He felt the marrow in his femur and heard a clicking sound that reminded him of pellet.

marrow

We all have marrow in our femur. It's not a plight and perhaps even conducive to a certain way of living. Tent-like. Or house-like. Possibly vine-like. Sometimes Tunta, despondent over his lack of tribute, played like he didn't get it. It wasn't believable, of course, because everybody gets it. Sometimes they go. Dress willy, for example. Or salt. And then there's the whole story of the shop sign. About how in future history books (or dictionaries), the word 'rose' will come to mean 'slab' or 'dark terror of stone'. But that's the future.

For now: to every traveler, a place to rest.

Ingomar

When Jaja found the head near the post of the wooden fence that separated the jungle from the road, the mouth on the head had a smile on it, which made Jaja think that the person who belonged to the head, smiled when the end came. Not true. You see, all that rolling along the road, hitting rocks and twigs and just your usual defects on a road that goes from city to country warped the old man's head so that it looked like there was a smile on his face. But no, he wasn't smiling when the end came.

what once was, no longer is

There are explanations for most--what shall we call them? --occurrences. But *what once was, no longer is* requires a more erudite explanation than usual. It was a foreshadower.

Martin wanted to take the taxi with the news girl to the river. Not with Sasha. Sasha worked at the shop. The news girl's leg is what Martin turned around to look at before he walked into the shop. The news girl and her leg came in later. Sasha, on the other hand, didn't show her leg. She did, however, show the back of her head, most of her forehead and part of her face. Martin didn't see any of Sasha so he sat down at a table and looked through the window. It was then that he saw the news girl walking towards the shop and children running across the road behind her. It was only when the news girl came into the shop that Martin noticed Sasha. But he got up and moved to the balcony so that when the news girl left, he left with her.

sondrine

Everyone knows the headlines. But are people aware of what's buried in the newspaper? The old man understood the print. The texture. But most of all he understood that it was the crinkly sound and the tiny little holes of the paper that revealed the details. Most headlines were uninteresting. D'Artagnan retired. Eliza Farthingbottom wrangled cattle in stilettos.

But the old man listened to his newspaper. First he spied the holes to see how it should be played and then he slowly began to turn sections of the newspaper in his hand until he had gotten every last crinkly sound out of it. He could tell you what was what when what wasn't obvious. So he wasn't worried about a damn thing when he finally put the newspaper down beside him.

glass

Martin looked through the window. He saw the news girl standing in the middle of the road. With his index finger he traced the outline of her body on the glass. He traced the traffic light beside her. Above her head he drew a small circle for the sun.

how things are hidden

The boy came from behind a palm tree near the river. He dashed over to the fence, naked and dripping wet, and picked up the head that lay near the fence post. He took the head with him and jumped back into the water and swam to the bottom of the river before making his way past the giraffe and owl, past the news girl shouting, past Martin on the balcony, past the helicopter, past the rose, past the fence, past the umbrella, past Sasha and the washboard, past the sun and the noise and the glistening of traffic until he found the old man. He swam over to him and placed his head back onto his body. And then he took the hat from the chair and placed it on his head.

The old man's eyes opened for a moment and then he hunched over to go back to sleep. On the brim of his hat written in small letters was the word *finito*.

Sean Brijbasi

The Sun is the Monster Eye

People think that I am dumb because I haven't had much to say for a long time. But I have been saving up my moments and hiding them behind my 'hello's and 'how are you's. I spoke little and wrote little, instead keeping notes on other people's moments and sometimes speaking of them as if they were my own.

The woman on the phone wants Christmas lights put up around the house before she gets home. She's going to stop by the store and buy those flowers. Those red flowers. I think she called them rhododendrons. She called the person on the other end of the phone James. She drew circles on her note pad while she was talking.

I don't know what to make of other people's moments. I keep thinking that one day I will open my notebook that I've filled with them and find the pages blank. I read them over and over again because they are almost invisible to me and shivery to my touchicles like they are hidden behind a thin sheet of ice. But I've collected enough of my own moments now and I feel the urge to relate them. Not for the purpose of having people see them or hear them. I don't really want them to. But my moments are running out of room in here and I don't have anywhere else to put them

Sew dresses Sasha. Don't do anything else.

You'll just have to decide if it's the right thing for you. She said she didn't know. They were quiet for a few blocks. The man's arm brushed against the woman's arm. Twice. Then they walked into an office building.

I finally arrive at Sasha's and I am bursting to tell her something. I knock on her door. I know she is in there but I call to her as if I am not sure. She doesn't mind that I pretend in this way because she says that I pretend in my own way.

It's raining here, but the sun is still visible in the distance. I feel naked in this rain and I feel that the sun is watching me.

I worry now because I wonder if anyone noticed that something fell from my pocket as I was taking my hand out. Flow. Maybe no one (er.) noticed but I have to be more careful. My urges are polarized.

"Sasha."

And then she comes out after a few moments, wearing a dress she has made of squares and flowers, a fusion of geometry and botany and biology. She tells me that her armoire is a circle, and her foot is a square, which is a flower, which is an eyelid that has yet to bloom. She tells me that they are and I believe her. She says that she will show me the proofs very soon.

"Okay," I say.

I tell Sasha okay from time to time because okays are good hiding places. The first step I take implies my long stride and impatience.

"Wait," she says.

She sees how strange the day is. Better than me. She says she sees well because of a child-hood catastrophe (insert insect) that destroyed her pupils (insert tacheon). She says she sees the molecules that make up a circle. She says that all circles are not the same.

"The sun is trying to hide now," she says. "It is hiding a little, but it is still there. And there are so many greens. Yes. So many that I can only see them if I don't think of them."

The pumas are migrating. Sew dresses Sasha.

I remember when Sasha thought a fish was a fish and not a disconnected tongue without fins. She says she knows better now. And yet she says, one day she will know more.

"What are you doing?" she asks me.

I don't know what she is talking about and I think that something has created an impasse between Sasha and myself. Sasha and me. Sasha and I. She asks me what I am doing and I don't know what she is talking about.

But I know the sun is watching. Latitudes display particular motions in congress. And sometimes progress.

"Slow down," she says.

And I do. I've seen others do it.

"Your eyelid is blooming," she says. "Don't you feel it?"

I feel nothing. I can't think of any other words that describe this feeling better.

I'd like to go to the bar and have a glass of whiskey, but Sasha still hasn't moved after our first step. I am a half-breed ahead of her and the space between us vibrates the theory of perpendicularity.

Auxiliary note: the theory of perpendicularity states that from any one axis, any point in time (past or future) can be mapped at different degrees along other axes in multiple dimensions. Future points and past points cannot be mapped on the same axis. End.

The vibrations are reaching my nodes. A husband is going to Montreal for the weekend.

"Sasha," I say, "can we hurry along?"

I say it normally because I want to have a drink and a cigarette. I want to watch my smoke explode against the bottom of an empty glass. I want to dance like my hole card is an ace.

I'm going all in.

While I wait for Sasha to catch up, I am propositioned by a vacancy. I enter like someone who he

Sits in a chair. Maps. Medulla oblongata. Sssssssssssss. Dust.

Sasha has caught up to me now and we continue to the bar. The relative ease of our stroll makes me think about balance and the fundamental flaw that is the essence of bipedism (insert name).

"Sasha," I say.

Sasha's dress is made of circles and flowers and things that I have seen her pick up in different places.

But I had noticed something that will be of help. While I was standing there I saw the same man over and over again. He seems to be walking around the blo(ck) {interesting note on model airplane #3} over and over again. I map a point to a previous past on another axis. I have a secret.

Some pasts are current.

We reach the bar and sit down at a table. I position my head at a forty-five degree angle to the wall beside us.

The circles were not perfectly drawn and some were colored in.

"Sasha," I say, "I am really bursting to tell you something."

"Tell me," she says.

Light travels along a random spine and finds its way into the bar.

"The sun is the monster eye," I say.

I start drawing circles on a napkin and my eyelid explodes. Petals float to the table. Sasha rubs the side of her glass. At another table someone is looking at us and writes something into a notebook. Everything stops.

Wayne Bowman

Sour Milk

At first I dreaded the weekly bath that came along with rich living. I was sure that, of all the mothers of the seven families who shared that bathroom, mine was the only one that ever took the time to clean it. She sanctified the big claw foot tub with Clorox every Saturday night just before she marched us down the hall for a bath, whether we needed it or not. In her zeal to keep us clean, she nearly scrubbed our skin off.

We had moved in and out of day rooms when we could afford it, but I had a feeling that, this time, my mother was going to make sure it was permanent. The room we rented was high dollar. There was a gas stove in one corner, a sink in another, a big bed along the wall on the other side of the room, and a table with four chairs between it and the stove. At the end of the room, a fold-down Murphy bed was built into the wall. For another twenty-five cents a day, we could have had an icebox, but my dad wouldn't hear of that.

By the time I was ten, I despised Cross so much that I plotted ways to kill him. Often times when I thought of Edith, I had to hide out in the bathroom for fear someone would see me and make fun of the huge bulge I got in my pants when I did. Between what my brother and his friends called "thrashing the monster," and thinking of Edith, I plotted ways to do away with Cross.

At the climax of one of my bathroom sessions, it struck me that I could drop something out the window onto his head, so I watched every day to see when he usually got home. After several days I discovered it was always at the same time, give or take five minutes either way.

I got a jar of my mom's pickled beets and set it on the windowsill. The first day I put it close to the edge, hoping it would fall of its own accord. That night he knocked Edith senseless and left her cuffed tight to the stove while he went on a drunk.

I spent the next day in the bathroom plotting how I would kill him until I was so exhausted that I had to sleep for several hours. At the end of the day I got up and found an iron skillet and made it teeter, still afraid to take responsibility for the murder I longed to commit. That night I watched through the fire escape window as he held her face down in a pan of dishwater until she passed out.

The next day I hid in shame because I was too much of a coward to help Edith. I intended to play hooky again and hatch a real plan to kill Cross. When I got to the bathroom the light was already out. I just figured the bulb was blowed, which was okay by me because I didn't want it on anyway. I locked the door and began one of my planning sessions, and right at the crucial moment, I was shocked to hear stifled laughter. My God, I wasn't alone. Oh, Jesus! Everyone would know I was a pervert.

"Who's there? I got a knife."

With that, Janie Igner twisted the bulb. There I was with my pants and underwear around my ankles and my pecker in my hand. To make matters worse, she wasn't alone. A red-faced Peggy Cherry stood not three feet away gawking at my crotch. I was mortified, but Janie had a strange look on her face that made me nervous. As I jerked at my pants she strode across the room and checked my frantic hands.

"It's okay. We won't tell nobody." She turned to Peggy who still hadn't moved.

"Will we Peg?"

Peggy made a low groan, but did not move. Janie had her hands on my arms to prevent me from getting my pants up, and in a soothing voice she whispered, "Let me see it."

I struggled hard to get away, but Janie wouldn't let me go, and to my surprise, Peggy joined her and they both held on to me until the tug-of-war made us all fall on the floor. As the struggle ensued, they began to giggle, and so did I. I finally gave up and let them have their way with me. Between bursts of laughter, they got my pants back down around my knees and put their faces very close to my pecker.

I drew the line when Peggy tried to touch it. I clamped my hands over it and did not loosen my grip until Janie said, " What will it take to let us touch it?"

I froze in fright, but began to think of what I wanted to let them examine IT. There was a long silence before I broke it with what I thought was the most original thought ever uttered. "I want to see yours."

They looked at each and giggled loudly.

I blurted out, "I want to see them both."

They stopped laughing and turned with the same weird look on their faces. Janie didn't hesitate for a second. She was out of her bloomers in a heartbeat, but Peggy did not move. When Janie jumped her, I joined in immediately and we wrestled Peggy's drawers down to her ankles. There I was, face to face with Peggy's peeper. After a little bit, she stopped struggling and I got a real good look, and as if she felt left out, Janie raised her skirt so I could see hers too.

For some reason Janie got on top of me and pushed me down on Peggy. We lay there in a ball for a good two hours. At one point Janie got to moaning, and I started breathing hard, and Peggy got to gasping for breath. It was the strangest, most exciting experience of my life though all we really did was lay there on each other. When it was all said and done, I felt like a guilty limp rag. Janie finally got up and pulled Peggy out from under me. They hunted around until they found their panties, and after Janie looked to see that the coast was clear, they left. I didn't get up until there was a knock on the door. It was my mother, who asked me if I was sick. I said I was and she helped me off to bed.

When I woke up that afternoon I was in time to fling my mom's biggest iron stew pot at Edith's old man. I don't know if it was dumb luck or good aim, but it clanged as it glanced off of the top of his head. Though there was a lot of blood and commotion as they carried him upstairs, he didn't die. At least he was laid up for a week, which gave Edith some time to heal. Lucky Mom didn't use that pot much.

I heard them fighting shortly after Edith nursed him back to health, and I went out on the fire escape to peek into their room. With the windows open to catch the summer breeze, I could hear everything. She was naked again and he was beating the hell out of her when I jumped in through the window. I grabbed her heavy iron that was still plugged into the light socket and when he turned to confront me, I cracked him in the head. I dazed him but he cold cocked me before I could hit him again.

While I was out, I had a series of disturbing dreams that had Janie and Peggy urging me to put my head up under Edith's skirt and take a good look at a big peeper. I woke up later back at my place with a busted nose. As my mother cradled me she said, "You're too little to get between a growed man and his wife. That'll get you kilt."

My dad whispered, "Next time use that Louisville Slugger you got for your birthday."

While Edith's husband beat her again later that night, he shouted, "I'll kill that little bastard if I ever catch you with him again." He screamed every vile name he could think up while he gave her another savage beating. It was weeks before she could come out in the daylight.

She never came out on the fire escape again. When I went to knock on her window, the shades were pulled, and she didn't bother to acknowledge that I was even there. She never came over again, and she began crossing the street to avoid me.

About the time her bruises healed and the bandages came off, I noticed she began to sneak out when Cross was at the bars. She got all painted up and put on tight sweaters, ironed her hot-pink pedal pushers and began to frequent beer joints in the red-light district. Over the next couple of years, I often saw her letting men feel her up and slobber all over her when I was out on the streets, shining shoes. Those same men began to follow her home as she staggered out of the late-night dives along the strip. At first they just felt her up, kissed her hard, and fondled her breasts and ass, but then they started stopping in the alley next to our building to take turns banging her up against the wall. I tried to get Dad to help her, but he said they weren't really hurting her and made me go to bed.

Cross was too chicken-shit to confront the men, so he contented himself with beating her after they stumbled off home. I guess she figured she might as well do what she was accused of if she had to take the beatings for it.

I got so jealous I wanted to hit her myself. Her husband finally gave her one last good pounding that would have landed him in jail again if he hadn't run off. Before he left he pronounced her a worthless whore to everyone who would listen.

From then on her door was always open to everyone but me. There was a man every night, sometimes two and three. I grew to hate the sounds she made with the new men more than I did the sounds of the beatings her old man had given her. I often sneaked over to watch the men she brought home rut and grunt on top of her. I was shocked by the violence of the act, and then I was fascinated. Was that what men and women really did together?

My mother finally caught me and pronounced me a "filthy little peeping tom!"

That was the only time she ever used the razor strap on me, and I never peeped again when she could have caught me. The bigger Edith's client list got, the more my imagination went wild with writhing bodies doing things I couldn't quite understand. The sounds that came through the walls drove me so mad with jealousy that I thought I would go out of my mind. I had to make her stop!

I waited one night until all of the erotic noises died in groans. When I was sure my family was asleep, I got out of bed; put on my clothes, coat and gloves; and went out onto the fire escape. I watched at the window until the man she was with threw some money on the bed and left. I waited to be sure he was gone before I quietly opened the window and crept into the room. I watched her for the longest time, hoping she was asleep, thinking of what she had become.

I stripped silently, and after hesitating for a while, I climbed in next to her. She opened her eyes slowly, expecting one of her johns. A flicker of shock came over her, but then she did a curious thing. She smiled and kissed me in a new way. I had trouble catching my breath. I kissed her back again and again and that night I finally knew why those men were anxious to pay her to rut around with them. I could not believe what I felt as I lay there spent.

After a little while she pulled my face up and looked into my eyes, but that smile disappeared in revulsion as she pushed me away violently. Shame flooded my mind and paralyzed my body. After a moment of indecision, I pushed my way back into the bed, and she shoved me out onto the floor, glaring at me. I made one last attempt to get back into the bed but she shoved me again and screamed, "Get dressed and get out!"

I obeyed. When I was fully dressed right down to my gloves, I turned to look at her for what I somehow knew would be the last time. As she lay there with her eyes closed, I remembered something my dad said to me about the squirrels we caught before he put them out of their misery.

"It's cruel to let them suffer."

That phrase echoed in my mind as I picked up the cold iron, which Edith had used so often, and brought it down on her head. Her startled eyes opened then closed slowly as she seemed to smile at me again. I was sure she was inviting me to end her misery? I hit her so many times that I lost track, then after I don't know how long, I stopped and put the iron down. I took off my gloves so I could touch her one last time. The warmth I had always known with her turned to the icy cold of death as I held her.

I could not bear to leave her until I had cleansed her of the filth that had been ground into her life. I washed her blood-matted hair, and I bathed her clear, white skin from her temples to her slender feet. No one, I was determined, would be able to say she had been dirty. I changed the bedclothes, put her in the dress she had worn to be baptized and left her, finally, at rest.

It was still dark when I eased myself off the bed and let her hands lie where they fell. I climbed back out onto the fire escape and went down to the basement boiler room. After taking off all my bloody clothes and burning them in the furnace, I sneaked, naked, up the stairs into the bathroom to wash myself. I made it back to our room without anyone ever knowing what I had done.

Several days later the landlord used his passkey to open her door when neighbors complained of the smell coming from her apartment. The women at the factory took up a collection; with that and her discount, Edith was buried in a fine casket lined with pink satin.

The cops took as many statements as they could get from normally tight-lipped neighbors. The ones who would talk testified that Cross had beaten Edith regularly ever since their baby had died and that lately she had begun to whore around. After a quick, sloppy investigation, the police pronounced it murder and arrested her husband. The newspapers printed lurid pictures of the crime scene and the headlines echoed in the judge's verdict that it had been a "crime of passion."

In the winter we put all of our food in a wooden box outside the window. The rats couldn't get at it there, but the damned squirrels drove my mother crazy until my father started trapping them. When snared, they made horrible noises until my father cracked them in the head with a ball-peen hammer he kept by the window. He said it was the merciful thing to do.

I was surprised at how much they looked like rats when they were skint out, though they tasted pretty good. Tasty as they were, I got tired of fresh squirrel meat and cornmeal gravy every night. At the end of a summer of sour milk and spoiled meat, Dad grudgingly gave up the extra two bits for the icebox. High living had a price.

Around daylight every morning the iceman sang out in a clear voice that roused us from our beds. I loved going down with my brother, lard bucket in hand, to get the daily nickel blocks of ice. While he got the ice, I scrambled around with the other kids catching chips caused by the pick the ice monger used to separate the blocks. After we emptied the water from the night before and delivered the block to the bottom of the icebox, we shared the shards of ice that were mostly cold water in the bucket by the time we got around to them.

My folks left for work before we woke, so after we got the ice, we reported to our next-door neighbor for powdered doughnuts and chocolate milk before we set off for school. Edith was easily the prettiest girl I had ever known. She was my mother's best friend, and she took care of us during the day when we were off from school. I thought her kind and gentle nature made her seem strangely out of place, and for someone who had a tragic past she was surprisingly happy. Her radiance softened the meanest people when she turned her smile on them. That radiance served as armor against everyone except her husband. It made no sense to me the way he beat her every night. She had married Lester Cross the year before last when she was fourteen. It embarrassed me, but I had a crush on Edith.

At first she didn't work except to take care of me, but after a while my mother got her a job at the casket company. I missed her, but I got to see her everyday after school when my brother and I walked down to the factory with a hundred other kids to wait for our moms to get off work.

During the daily parade the women walked and gossiped and their children played and fought along the few blocks back up to heart of the inner city. At first the other kids teased me because I liked to hold Edith's hand more than I liked to play with them, but they gave it up after a while.

When we got home on Fridays, we waited for the ice cream man to ride up on his bicycle. He always had a good supply of Popsicles and drumsticks. It was a tradition with my Dad that we got ice cream every Friday, and if the other kids were lucky, Dad was drunk and he bought one for anybody who got in line. Once he made the mistake of buying one for Edith. When the cold made her nipples hard I felt myself flushing as I stared at them. As I turned away I realized every man on the street had been staring. Word got back to Cross I guess, because he beat her up so bad she couldn't go to work for a week.

Every time someone whistled at Edith, she got a beating, and no matter how hard she tried to hide her good looks, she couldn't. Once Cross beat her so badly that she was laid up for a month and the cops took him off to the workhouse. The judge gave her a thirty-day vacation from the son-of-a-bitch.

When Edith got evicted because she couldn't pay the rent, my mother took her in and nursed her back to health. Though my brother grumbled about it, I didn't mind that my mother gave Edith the Murphy bed as long as I got a pallet on the floor next to her. I often woke up in the night and watched her silhouetted body quiver through her nightclothes as she stood in the moonlit window crying.

In return for my mother's hospitality, Edith watched over me again. She didn't eat until I was full, and she used the little money she had tucked away to buy me treats at the corner candy store. The last thing I did at night was reach out to hold her hand, and I forced myself to wake up early so I could watch her sleep. It got so I preferred to cuddle with her on weekends rather than my family.

Edith's husband got out of jail, and word got around that he was a changed man. It wasn't long before he came sniffing around again like an old horny dog. He found out that Edith was with us and came one night to beg forgiveness. He swore a thousand oaths to God that he would never lay hands on her again. After a week of hard groveling she took the worthless piece of crap back. As promised, he was true to his word --- for almost a whole week. From then on the beatings were less severe but more frequent. Before long it was back to business as usual though he was careful to stop short of a beating that would land him back in jail. The cops didn't mind if a man beat his wife as long as he didn't leave too many marks or kill her.

The first time I ever saw a naked woman was when Cross mauled Edith and threw her out into the hall without a stitch of clothes. I watched her with a sick fascination that stirred something inside me that I had never felt before. It made my stomach hurt, and shame overwhelmed me though I had only a vague idea why.

My mother sent my old man over to talk to Cross. I followed in the shadows to watch. It took Cross a while to answer the door, and when he saw who it was, he tried to slam it, but my old man put his shoulder against it, pinning Cross against the wall. My dad spoke in a low dangerous voice that I only heard when he was really mad. "My wife sent me over here to tell you that if you ever do that to Edith again I am to come over and kick the shit out of you, and that is exactly what I'll do." Old Cross who was struggling to catch his breath was shaken' like a dog shittin' razorblades. Dad growled, "You understand?" Cross waggled his head up and down from behind the door where he was trapped, and with that my dad let him go. Cross watched him until Dad got halfway to our place, then he slammed the door and shouted, "Kiss my ass!" Pop turned abruptly and headed for the door to Cross's apartment. When he got there, he didn't bother to knock; he just splintered door and after a struggle just out of sight, Cross flew out. The floor shook as he slammed into the wall across the wide hall. My dad followed and stood over him. "I don't think I made my point." With that he kicked the hell out of Cross. "This is my last warning!" While Cross was begging and crying for him to stop, I high-tailed it back to our place and waited for Dad. I was always proud of him, but never as much as I was that day.

There must have been some code of how far a man could go when beating his wife. The little talk my old man had with Cross must have worked because he never put her out in the hall again though we all knew he stepped up the abuse behind closed doors.

Dad always said, "He must be good in bed if she puts up with that shit." I had no clue what that meant when I nodded and returned his wink though, I figured, that must have been the only place where he was nice to Edith.

Cross, who was a sometime security guard, used an old pair of handcuffs to shackle Edith to the cook-stove in their room on Friday nights while he went out drinking. With the help of the fatback grease she kept on the stove, she usually slipped out of them and joined us on the fire escape where we talked and laughed the nights away. In the winter my mom made vanilla snow cream, which Edith loved. Mom even gave her the secret family recipe.

Edith was always careful to say please and thank you, and she made sure I got the last bite from her bowl. If the snow cream made me shiver, she was quick to wrap me in a quilt and warm me with her body, often kissing me to sleep. I grew to love Edith, and I think she loved me.

My mother whispered, "I wish her baby hadn't died. It would have been a comfort to her."

"What did it die of?"

"Her milk soured and poisoned it. "

"Why didn't she get milk from the store?"

"Her man told her they didn't have no money to waste on store-bought milk."

"Too bad she didn't give him some of that poisoned milk."

Mom gave me a half-hearted, "Now," to show her Christian nature.

Edith always sat with us while Mom went out to search for my old man when he went on a drunk. That usually took half the night. We often went over to her room when my brother was gone out with his friends. She ironed clothes and I played. The iron was old and heavy as lead, and it wore her out as she used it to put the razor-like creases in her husband's pants. When she got tired, we cuddled up next to one another in her big chair and waited to hear "Love Me Tender" on the hit parade before we drifted off to sleep. I began to doze in dreams that I was afraid to recall in the daylight. I don't know how she managed it, but I always woke up back in my own bed.

Terri Carrion

Catholic School Retablos

I stand at my locker, fifteen and bound in a white starched shirt, red acrylic wool vest and a gray gabardine uniform skirt with an obscene pleat straight down the front. I can see Sister Nulla sliding up the hall, Jesus on a giant wooden crucifix hanging from her neck, his nailed feet bouncing against her hidden breasts. Sister's thin, translucent fingers are interlaced, hands cupped right below Jesus as if she's about to give him a boost up to Heaven, the way my father gave me a boost out of the pool at the YMCA, where the water was always murky and green like Sister Nulla's eyes.

In Algebra class, Sister Catherine tries to get our attention by whipping the blackboard with her pointing stick. Her face shrivels, eyes bug out of their slots as she paces back and forth, screaming, picking out students to expel to the hall as chalk dust hovers in the air around her. Formulas blur. Dust floats, sparkles, settles on Sister's forehead like ash.

At lunch, while our classmates gather at the sub shop down the street, Lisa and I sit alone on the grass in Senior Square in front of the white statue of the Virgin Mary and eat sunflower seeds making sure to save a handful to bury at her feet. We want something to grow. Spread across the concrete. Burst from the cracks like sunrise.

The infirmary fills up faster than confession during Easter. Girls fake fainting to escape the 14 stations of the cross, the claustrophobic chapel, the kneeling and standing and sitting and kneeling—hours of it— the monotone chanting, those carved wood scenes of Jesus falling, falling, falling and Father in his purple robe, the stained glass behind him glowing like fire. By station 5, the girl's thighs begin to twitch. Not from the thought of eternal damnation, but from the looks the boys give as they wait for the girls to collapse, one by one, plaid skirts rising, rising, rising.

When the school gym is vandalized right before Christmas, Sister Hortencia howls, runs through the brick courtyard to the principle's office and leaves the gym doors wide open. A gust of stink like the pier hits us. Noses pinched we peek in. See silvery fish the size of footballs scattered across the red floor, piled atop the gold painted warrior, dangling from the basketball hoops, hundreds of them, glimmering beneath the streams of morning sun like a miracle.

Surprise confession. I'm called out of class to see Father Campion. He sits behind his giant oak desk, his face bloated and pink from too much wine. The walls are covered with posters of Mexican bullfights, black beasts in tortured positions, their flesh pierced and bleeding, like Jesus on the cross, who shares the walls with the bulls and matadors. And I wonder about Father, his need to display all this unnecessary sacrifice and how *matador* means killer in Spanish. Father wants me to confess. Can't think of anything I'm sorry for so I lie, tell him I sometimes imagine stabbing my mother in the neck with her knitting needles. I receive my penance. Say my Hail Mary's in a flash. Get back to art class where I learn perspective, try to capture shadow and light.

Ira Cohen

Ferry to Xania

It's already July 11th, around 4 A.M. We are on *The Aptera*, bound for Crete. The sky and sea mirror each other in total darkness. Even the North Star has disappeared. I am on the top deck. Almost no one is still here among the rows of bright orange plastic chairs held fast to the deck in rows of twelve. I cannot sleep because my lap is Lakshmi's pillow. I have been reading *VALIS* by Philip K. Dick. "The Empire Never Ended," he writes as Horselover Fat. He has me going in circles with his theological arguments, his corollaries — "1. Those who agree with you are insane. 2.Those who do not agree with you are in power." Then "1. Some of those in power are insane. 2. And they are right."

I listen to the hum of the ship's motors. Like the airplane heading for Romania, the ship seems to be still & humming — not moving, since not even a cloud is visible. Now the radios & tape recorders have been shut off. Before a Greek song mixed with the infernal humming gave an impression of a haunting voice calling the world to prayer. I thought of Subbulakshmi singing the songs of Meera. Imagine such a ferry, grand as this one with its reflective silver ceilings below decks, floating in space — devotional songs coming over the loudspeakers. Suddenly it is timeless & although we are mostly asleep, some remain awake writing in notebooks or prowling the deck in shawls or capes held at the throat. There goes someone with a large yellow towel. A woman sits alone smoking a cigarette. Now she holds herself. A soldier looks down at the foam churned up by the boat. Dinner is long over and now we are pilgrims, voyagers once again, while the crowds stay hidden below decks.

Now Lakshmi is my table. She looks up drowsily for a moment & says, "I love you, daddy." "Go back to sleep, my little table. Can't you see that your pillow is writing?"

Josh Davis

Where is My Mind?
(from "Under the Blue Banner of Heaven")

When I finally get back to Alton, I take full advantage of my jet lag and move immediately into a small house on the outskirts of town with a few old and relatively warm-blooded friends.

Henry, once an eightieth level barbarian and semi-professional psychotropic preacher, is now a thinly spread and occasionally balding volatile stress insurgent enrolled in post graduate studies at a local college. He is also as a part-time substitute teacher, horticulturalist, construction worker, drug addict, amateur beard farmer and is the perennial father-figure of the house. He greets me at the door with the slightest hint of eyelids, wearing a beat up old pair of blue jeans that is loose even on his husky frame, and the same green Grateful Dead shirt he's been wearing since I met him a hundred and fifty three years ago.

"Charlie! Welcome home, brother. Come on in."

"Henry. That's really a lovely scent you're wearing. What's it called?"

"Sweat, cheap beer, and marijuana. It's French, I think. Do you really like it?"

"Oh, it's lovely. You'll have to tear me a page out of the magazine some time."

James Watson is sitting in the same hole in the center of the couch that he's been working on for as long as I've known him. By day he is a pharmacist, and by night he is less noble, but equally qualified. His cousin, a cook at a local Red Lobster, is sitting exactly four inches away from the television. I wonder if he's waiting to be beamed off the planet. The circles under his eyes are just a few feet smaller than The Grand Canyon.

The town, Alton, is now threatening to become something beyond the mere specter of a city it once was—now injected with large chain video stores, brand name restaurants, over-priced coffee shops, designer furniture stores, plush air conditioned sixteen screen luxury stadium seated movie theaters, and fashionably empty martini bars.

But the people have remained the same. The mood has remained the same, even if the dress code has gone semi-casual.

"Hey Henry, do I have to wear a tie to watch Mars Attacks on cable?"

I think it's good to be back. I think I'm relieved. When you're away from any place for long enough, you start to miss the mundane comfort of everyday absolute boring certainty. If this is the best the welcoming committee can do, I will take it. I am free, happy, and light.

. . . .

My neighbor drives a White Car.

The inside of her house is a post-tornado collage of clothes, food wrappers, beer cans, cigarettes, and dishes covered with mold older than I am. She is twenty, and she is lovely.

Also, I have the secret suspicion that she is pure evil.

A spiral bound draft of my second novel that I had made specially and for more money than I care to comment on sits on a shelf in her living room like the farthest, smallest, coldest star in space.

Late at night she tells me she wants to be a muse and tosses her hair and blinks like she's trying to tear Odysseus from his roped position at the mast. She has a lazy, easy loveliness about her. It might be the drugs, or the lighting. But in the twilight of the room, every trivial idiotic thing she says is absolutely captivating. You trust her deep brown eyes like you would trust a dog's eyes. You watch her lips part with malevolent glee and count the microscopic beads of sweet on the nape of her perfect swan-like neck with curious grave envy.

Sometimes I listen to her. When we are alone she likes to talk about the stereotypes surrounding small towns and all her wild ambition to be something large that contains multitudes. When we are not, she talks about how "fucked up" or "wasted" she, or someone in her company was the previous night. She talks about these things with the loud optimism of someone watching a football game, like she's trying to keep score. She tells me how determined she is to lead the league in liver damage, lung cancer, and brain cell extinction.

"We call that the triple crown," I tell her.

She blinks twice and continues. I am senselessly captivated.

Timothy Lloyd walks in the room, smokes something, nods, and leaves for work.

The White Car stretches out to reveal her midsection. I can tell, because my eyes have corners. I imagine watching this exquisite display is the modern day twenty-something equivalent to watching Moses part the Red Sea.

. . . .

Eve Saul knocks gingerly on the back door. I know it's her, because I've had ten years to learn that knock. I know her stealthy steady silent rhythm. I know she will wait for at least ten minutes before bothering to knock again, in case someone is sleeping, or about to achieve inner peace. I know her neck is craned and that she is peering through a small pane of glass into the darkness of the laundry room. I can see the splintering blue-silver light coming off her eyes, and I'd make a two-to-one bet that she's humming quietly to all the lucky crickets in the backyard. I know a lot of things about her, and she probably knows even more about me. I know that she, conversely, is anything but evil.

I open the door and she comes in with a ridiculously bright grin that I am convinced was erected solely for my benefit.

She sits on a small couch in my room and tells me about work. She is telling me that she cannot believe people do things and participate in whatever ordinary imperfect human actions people participate in on a daily basis. Like, the other day someone coughed during a meeting. Imagine! I smile and glance down at the floor so as not to let on that I too am imperfect and human and ordinary. In ten years, this seems to be the one thing she hasn't figured out about me, or, moreover, about the world—that we are all miserably imperfect. I smile, and I glance down at the floor because I am the unhappy king of miserably imperfect.

. . . .

I live indoors.

Tim is attempting to type a paper about a short story he couldn't care less about. The computer trembles under his short stubby shivering fingers. Henry is taking a shit six feet away. We can hear him singing broken Marvin Gaye and Tenacious D songs through the wall. A thin film of brown featherdust drops backwards off the ceiling.

The White Car pulls up next door. We watch her through the window with imaginary x-ray glasses. Her slinky paper doll figure flutters across the dirt driveway towards a broken screen door that might be a misplaced prop from a Tim Burton movie. For a moment, I imagine I can actually hear her high girlish voice raise an extra octave to greet the silky arched back of her cat.

"Man."

"I know. Yeah."

"Where was I?"

"*The Yellow Wallpaper.* You need a middle paragraph, an educated conclusion, a few sources, a topic sentence, a basic assumption as to theme, and then you're practically finished."

"Right. How do you spell *wallpaper*?"

"The *H* is silent."

Tim sighs and goes back to typing. The computer barks and chews up its own tail.

Through the wall we hear the shower start and the singing continue. I start to pace. I am wondering about fast food restaurants.

Chicken or beef? Taco Bell? Pizza? A loaf of bread and a pound of roast beef, ketchup and a twelve pack of coke? I wonder if the mail has come yet.

Henry walks out of the bathroom, no longer with misplaced broom hair or ripped Miller High Life t-shirt. I'm a little disappointed, and I tell him so.

We fix Tim's margins and center the title over his topic sentence. I wonder if I should listen to music?

. . . .

I had thoughts once. I'm laughing at the dead prospect of ghost thoughts.

I like the sound the ceiling fan makes, even though it keeps me awake. To me, it sounds like progress. Something in my room is spinning clockwise.

I'm happy with the temperature today. This is something. I walk outside and stare straight up as if to thank the clouds. I look next door to see The White Car that spills slinky things that flutter and dissipate.

Inside, on the counter, are beer footprints and unwrapped phantom cheeseburger castles.

"Someone should really take that shit out." The ceiling fan whirs.

"Fuck off."

"What's up, man?"

A leper and a little dog appear. "Nothing. Nothing. Nothing."

I wonder if I'm getting enough sleep. I wonder if there is enough iron in my diet. I wonder if listening to the rhythm of your own heartbeat is detrimental to its progress.

The walls at the base of my bed are cool and hypnotizing. I pick at pillows and pull at dreams even though my eyelids are painted sun-green.

There're a thousand things I should do. Talk to people. Go places. Eat. Shit. Sing. Woody Allen once said, "eighty percent of life is just showing up." I think he said "eighty." I don't care. I could kick Woody Allen's ass.

Sometimes the phone rings and is answered before the caller ID can pick up. Sometimes it rings for days, despite twelve hands on six phone lines.

I should really clean my room. License plates and oil crayons and wrapping paper two months late. Socks and tissues, unrelated. Cds and empty popcorn bags.

Instead, I watch the deleted scenes from "Lost in Translation."

. . . .

Are midgets funny?

Tim is complaining about midgets not being funny. He doesn't like things that make him uncomfortable, like midgets, centennial porn, the word *cul-de-sac*, or most forms of basic human interaction.

"What time is it?"

"Uh—six o'clock?"

"Hmm. What day?"

It's Tuesday. In grade schools, they taught us colors. Blue days are for music class. Yellow days are Phys Ed.

The television is debating the political future of mannequin orangutans. Henry is debating a fifth hit of marijuana. I'm debated the merits of the pill bottle in my jacket pocket.

Tim is fidgeting. Tim is very good at fidgeting. Besides this, he has an astonishing center of gravity which he often uses to topple those taller than him, which is to say, everyone. His eyes are steady and also dog-like, only his are dog-like in an unflinchingly friendly way rather than being hypnotizing or sinister. You want to trust him when he mumbles desperation. You know that if you were ever truly desperate he would lay down in traffic if it would make the world right again.

Tim wants to hit up a bar. I'd like to find my legs. Henry wants to follow the yellow brick road and sing about the more off-beat uses of maple syrup.

The phone rings and no one answers it.

· · · · · · · · · ·

Sometimes things come in the mail. I put on my least conspicuous hat and walk gingerly by the ghost-White Car, across the street to the box. Dead people get more mail than I do. I'm serious. I'm contemplating faking my own death to see if they'll posthumously award me a Sears catalogue.

Cars purr by and forget to wave. I keep my head down, because I've seen too many old movies.

Inside, it smells like burnt doll hair. I run my hand through my own closely-clipped mop and rub the tops of my eyelids.

During the day, everyone is either asleep or working. I pace the thirty yard track to the bathroom to do my daily reading.

I like the wallpaper in the bathroom. It imagine it would smell like the ocean if we ever mopped the floors or cleaned the counters or vacuumed or pulled the mountains of dead soapy hair out of the drain.

Sometimes I check the fridge. Still there. The phone rings and I take off my shoes.

. . . .

I drink another coke and lick my teeth. Still there.

. . . .

Little strips of paper remind me to do things. Call the car insurance company and tell them that existence precedes essence. Send that girl who works at the Virgin Megastore in Times Square the DVD of that music video you shot last summer. Finish formatting the margins of that short story about ironically idealistic Satanist midwifes. Find a more efficient path to clean socks.

When the outside lights click off, I pull the little beaded brass rope hanging from my heroic ceiling fan and make everything red. I wonder if the cars passing by think I'm running a brothel. I don't think I could really run a brothel. I'd probably be too busy giving idealistic lectures to the whores and patrons.

"Just buy her dinner."

"Just let him buy you dinner."

. . . .

I get an email from a girl I've never met. I send one to a girl without fingers. I call a girl I'll never sleep with. The White Car in the driveway next door disappears. Somewhere, a girl I'll never see again is laughing at me.

"That fucker."

I tell people it doesn't faze me anymore.

"Ahh, I've given up. It's not worth the sweaters."

They nod their heads and appear solemn, like winter wheat fields.

I'm addicted to my computer. It tells me who's on first, when the second sequel to the movie adaptation of the third extra's character in Ed Wood's forth film is coming out, and what I should think about the latest record by a British band that sounds a little like early Radiohead. The display screen tilts backward and imagines pebble rings in childhood rivers.

. . . .

The house sounds like rain at night. Things creek and cascade and scurry. I imagine it's just mice, but I hold out the hope that it's secretly the shallow footsteps of quasi-reformed prostitutes skulking around in tight Sonic Youth t-shirts.

When I open my eyes again, red is yellow.

Every morning still has shades of Christmas. Everything is possible. I lay perfectly still for a while and listen for hoof prints.

Realizing one can't *listen* for hoof prints, I make a motion for the remote.

Bombs! Death! Injury! Panic! Bus rides! Thirty-five degrees and partly cloudy!
Click.
Start getting real.
Click.
No he dihint!
Click.
Hold it. There's a kid out there. Tommy! Get out of there!
Click.
Well, it's a long story, but…
Click.
I'll do it. Whatever it is, I'll do it. I don't care. Whatever it…
Click.
Here's one of California's finest.
Click.
Only the best for…
Click.
Bombs! Death! Injury! Panic! Bus rides

. . . .

Sometimes I actually have dreams, and the buffet gets weird. The food isn't who it's supposed to be. Sometimes I wipe all the cobwebs off heaven, and it's suddenly morning.

I spend most of the day cleaning and shopping— stocking up on foods that might be deemed nourishing or beneficial, cooking a grand meal, and teaching a few beer cans how to disappear completely.

Today I replace the oppressive red lights in my ceiling with pale blue. It's a banner day, really. I wonder if I remember how to write a proper press release. I think the key is **VERY BOLD TYPE** and a great deal of exclamation points.

Later, I give up and instead run through the woods with the dog.

Later still, I wander a video store with Graham and Tim. We dive like cartoon superheroes through rows of sub par silver screen ejaculations until we find the perfect mix of pretentious art house fodder and achingly modern quasi cult horror movies.

Half doped and resembling one of the middle characters in the evolution chart, I lead the division towards a tall, beautiful, nymph-like waif slightly imperfect in completely acceptable places standing behind the cash register who instantly agrees with me on the achingly modern quasi cult horror movie—who I want to invite over for blue-lit red wine and discussions of infinite comma-less sentences about indefinable things and accidentally kiss and fall through the ceiling fan. I almost do it too. Hell, I'd propose if I thought she could fit in one of my shoes.

In the parking lot, we pass a red Honda civic with a Fugazi bumper sticker as it pulls up six spaces to our left. Lola Thomas—who I'd just had a beautifully unrealistic dream about two nights ago—who I almost wrote or called or telepathed—steps out and trots alone past us into the video store. I, barely in my car, honk the horn, wave and disappear.

All these dead things keep walking over my most famously irrepressible errors. I suddenly wish I'd invented street signs.

A good song comes on the radio, and I pretend I'm listening to every quarterbeat.

Back at the house we throw on the first movie as Graham invents a fog machine and Tim stencils himself into the back wall. Ten minutes later, just as vampires are discovering bullets, a girl walks in on Morticia Adams tentacles and says her and The White Car next door aren't doing anything and wonders if we'll relocate and watch the rest of the movie with them.

Graham and I skip rope across the nascent dewy backyard. Tim goes home.

I sit next to Morticia Adams, who is quite lovely, and is an unironic a Strokes fan.

"What does that have anything to do with…"

"Fuckoff."

"Who are you walking to?"

"Talking."

"You know what I mean."

The girl in The White Car produces a four-foot shoot of bamboo and starts a fire. I hold the flame for her and watch the screen door flood with migrant butterflies.

We trade places and I fall backwards into the nearest shadow of lamplight. My wings twitch, but don't flutter. I try to look like the perfect art-core mutilation of every movie paradox in the history of film. But instead I watch dumbly until the credits roll and go home invisibly to eat tacos with Kevin Shields.

The vapor and sea-saw movement of the ground glide through the nothingness of atoms, and the nothingness of humanity, and the nothingness of vapor thoughts hummed at drunken electronic sparrows. At my best moments I run into the most walls, where pure feeling equals existing and essence is only a mirror image of the accidents we arrange our lives over.

. . . .

I have a dream that Kirsten Dunst and I are sitting on top of the world making beautiful radioactive children. They all come out electric blue. Her eyes and my eyes are so iridescent and immediately striking together that people have instant epileptic fits.

Our enemies try to outlaw the colors we create—solid colors so pure—so wildly serene—we even make a black that gives out instant orgasms.

When I wake up, I am the fish with the bicycle again.

Now I'm just a little tired, too tired to have an actual "mood."

The other day I tried to tell a girl that liver damage is always the fastest way to a man's heart. My most redeeming qualities are often the ones most responsible for my utter ineptitude as a human being.

I'm bored with picnic tables. I suppose things just move in slow motion sometimes. Sometimes they stop.

All the places I've been—seen—all the history, it all means so very little to me now. The best things always happen like weatherman mistakes and cancel the world.

Being in Paris four years ago was awful with just one set of eyes, not to mention all the bread was stale. But coming back—falling asleep in the smallest room in Baltimore with a lone, kind, warm blooded loving and soft-hearted girl just killed off every river, palace, painting, or ballet broadcast memory possible. I have become obsessed by those dead memories. They're my own slow motion black and white film flashbacks, and I am the worst, most unshaven pathetic Humphrey Bogart character in the history of cinema.

It never felt right traveling, seeing all that beauty alone. I always felt too small for all that. I couldn't keep it all in. It's better here. It's easier to make sound where there is no sound. It's easier to hear when there is nothing to cover up the silence.

I'd rather be an unwritten encyclopedia entry. I'd rather stare at the back of someone's head than an eighth century castle.

It occurs to me that I'm both terrified of and in love with everything. I'm like a blood whore for a gang of emotional vampires. I'm romantically vitriolic. I dive headfirst and at light speed into piles of sand hoping I'll make something other than glass. I'm a bag or rocks waiting to be stereo circles in city street puddles. I'm the sound of abject patience painting the ground clear.

All I ever wanted to be was smiling light bulb wire.

. . . .

I wake up the next morning and write a goodnight letter to the queen of the Martian sandbox.

Later, someone's car takes me to a hardware store where I trade my legs for manic indifference.

The phone walks around, holding up old pictures and laughing. Other than that, the planet is quiet. A little dog lay at my side licking my hands. Its breath smells like a three day showerless summer. Its eyes flutter and reach. Sometimes it falls asleep and starts chirping at the wind and running in place.

. . . .

If someone asked me what I wanted these days, I wonder if I'd be able to answer without raining sarcasm. I wonder if I could fold up until I became light enough to fly. I wonder if my skin could grow through the wallpaper if I left it lying there.

Graham walks through the door and knocks.
   "Asshole!"
   "Hey!"
   "Come on in. There's a chair and an ice cube tray."
He takes the latter. His eyes spin silvery webs through his brain and crawl straight out. It's safe to say Graham has stopped taking unleaded. He pulls at his beard as if it was made of Velcro and could be yanked off and traded it for an out of print Nation of Ulysses record. He has eyes tattooed on his arms and I've never before asked him why.
   "Tim?"
   "Cough."
   "Right."
   We go to the post office, where they keep all the eyes that crawl out. The girl in front of us is about our age,

but she appears to be about three zeros more comfortable. Her hair is tied up in court, and her slender black skirt smells exactly like her beach house.

An old man behind us makes bitter old man jokes. Graham's skin cracks and flakes off on the floor.

Then everyone becomes featureless—first red and swollen—then pale to the point of translucence. The floor reflects on the ceiling.

"That's cheating."

"Can I help the next person?"

"Help! Help!"

Willie Davis

Gather and Sing

The last time my enormous, far-flung family all came together to gather and sing was on the Christmas Eve six months after my mother dropped dead of a stroke. It started simple enough. My father had us gather around the piano and my grandfather Clay took out his fiddle and they began belting out carols. Soon, the women started humming, and then the men. I may have been the last holdout, but by the time I started murmuring, everyone else was in full voice, trying to keep up with my father. He had such a strong voice that no one sang with him, only around him, like branches around a trunk.

In the middle of O Holy Night, my sister's voice broke, which set off my brother Jeff, my hysterical Aunt and me. I'm a graceless crier. Stoicism is beyond my grasp, even as an idea. I tried holding the sobs in, which made a tortured hiccup sound, and each corner of my face twitched to its own separate rhythm. When my family saw me, they all started crying too. The men cried louder than the women, because they were drunker and their voices were better suited to it, but the women weren't holding back. The chorus of crying made its own song, different but not inharmonious to the one my father sang.

Throughout it all, his voice never wavered. His fingers hit a few wrong keys, and his rhythm slowed, but his voice stayed strong as ever. Sometimes, I thought he was good at nothing except singing.

After he finished the song, he ran his hands through his hair, wiped his nose, and gave everyone a chance to catch their breath. "Jesus," he said. "Of all the times I've made my family cry, I think this might be my favorite." People laughed, relieved that he wasn't going to cry himself. Instead, he leaned back and cracked a big toothy grin. "How about an Irish one?" The women hollered and the men raised their drinks, as he leaned forward to lead us all in a chorus of:

Resemble Ol' Rosin the Beau, Boys,
Resemble Ol' Rosin the Beau
I hope that the next generation
Resembles Ol' Rosin the Beau.

My mother was Irish, and as much as she's still my mother, still is.

The men in my family outlive the women. It's not by design, it just happens that way. Most times we live hard, hurt ourselves in public, and stay primed for early death, but then, out of either bad luck or the wrath of

God, we survive well after the women have succumbed to strokes, coronaries, or the sorts of hard quick deaths that come by falling in a bathtub and breaking a hip after they're too old to heal.

My grandfather used to terrorize the town. When he was twenty-four, he beat a black man half to death with a lead pipe. The black man had a fractured skull, and two broken ribs. No one knew why, except they thought he was racist. That never seemed right. He was a racist, but he had an enormous sense of irony, and he even named his youngest son Martin Luther Clay, just to see the rise it got out of his friends. To him, names and children were just signposts: little footprints that showed the direction of his thoughts. Nobody who took life that loosely would take a pipe to a black man just because he was black.

He spent at least a year in prison, but not for what he did to the black man. My father said it was because he called the mayor's wife a whore, but my father lies. Uncle Frankie told me he cut a woman with a broken bottle. "Ask anyone," he said. "Teddy Clay's the meanest man in Kentucky." He said it with some pride and I could believe it except that the next morning, Frankie, severely hung over, couldn't remember saying it.

Hysterical Aunt Marie swore he was picked up in a conspiracy for arson. "He wanted to burn down city hall," she said between puffs of her endless string of cigarettes. "He'd have almost surely done it too, except he bought out the store's supply of kerosene, and the merchant got suspicious."

Maybe. Maybe he cut the mayor's whore and burned down City Hall to hide the evidence. No one knows who can tell it without apologizing, and that's why I don't ask him. He'd start out with an excuse or an apology, and by the time he was done telling it, he would honestly want my forgiveness. And I did want an apology, but not for that.

Before my grandmother, Nora, died, my grandfather had the coldest stare I've ever seen on anyone, man or beast. My cousins and I would run up to him and hug his legs, asking him questions and begging him to tell us stories. He would roll his head around in a full circle, always keeping his eyes steady on the one who'd been the loudest. Then, he'd flick his cigarette at us: too high to hit us, but close enough to make us scatter. If Jeff or one of the older cousins tried to prove they were brave by staying near him, he'd light another cigarette, smoke it halfway down, and throw it at them again, closer this time. "Ask me something else," he'd say, "if you want one in the ear."

Sometimes, he came home with new tattoos. His wife didn't ask him where he'd gotten them or what they meant, and God knows if she kept noticing after a while. Because after scores of physical changes he put himself through—tattoos, chipped teeth, fresh scars— he always looked the same. In every adult picture I've seen of him, he's bald, razor thin, and staring cock-eyed into the camera, like it's got something to prove.

Then, one day, his wife slipped on a patch of black ice while carrying her groceries, cracked her head, and was sent to the hospital for the last eight months of her life. They gave her the wrong medicine, and she never even halfway recovered. It's as freak a death as a car wreck, only slower.

After that he turned soft. He talked to his grandchildren when they approached him, and he even held the little ones. We lost our fear of him and soon lost our interest in him as well. He smiled more, but they weren't kind smiles. They were the desperate and practiced smiles of a rattled man: not a happy one.

My father was dangerous in a different way. He had the ability to believe every thought he had was the truth. This absolved him of his sins as far as he was concerned, because he simply had to want them gone and they would disappear. That opened up the world for him, and he used his absolution like a derringer, pointed towards the ones he loved. Once, when the alderman's twelve year old daughter ran away for a week, he called the police and told them his brother Terry had locked her in his basement. He meant it as a joke and assumed Terry would take it the same way, but Terry swore he'd never speak to him again. My father, sobbing and bent kneed, begged for forgiveness. "It was a joke," he kept pleading. "You know you're not a kidnapper. They know you're not a kidnapper." Terry forgave him within the hour. He didn't want to, but there was no other choice. He could beat him bloody or renounce his name, but he couldn't make my father understand what he did was wrong. He already understood—he'd just forget it as soon as he turned around. Terry knew—like the rest of us came to know—there was no other way to deal with an amnesiac except to forgive him.

He had a slew of women on the side and he never even tried to hide them. He took me to their houses, and introduced me to them. Some of the women fixed me lunch and set me up in front of the TV while they went at it in the bedroom, but some just looked away, embarrassed. My father was never embarrassed. He took me out for hotdogs almost every time after and said, "What's the one thing we have in common, you and me?"

I learned the answer he wanted. "We're the best looking men in Kentucky."

"You're goddamn right about that," he said. "Now get out there and tell somebody."

It's hard to say whether my mother forgave him or just let him forgive himself, but it all amounted to the same thing. She was older than him, less needy, and she'd already traveled across her ocean. She didn't need to retreat into her stories, and so she was happy coaxing her family along, cooking her ready-made meals, and smoking her oversized hand-rolled cigarettes. After the funeral, some women in the neighborhood started talking about how the stress of my father's affairs had weakened her. They said as much to me and I just smiled and nodded, half-suspecting it was true. My father didn't want to believe it, but once he heard them say it, he couldn't put it aside. That was the curse of his mindset. He could believe any lie he told was the truth, no matter how outlandish, but once an idea wormed its way into his head, he could never dismiss it, no matter how much it hurt. The second he heard the women talk about him, he knew he'd carry the guilt for good, like a terminal disease. Worse, this time he didn't want absolution.

So, by that Christmas Eve, six months after my mother's final stroke, he'd already begun to reshape himself. I could hear it in his stories. He no longer praised himself as the dirty prankster, who prized his jokes above his friends. Instead, he was an everyday joker, who could let a gag go too far, but only out of the most honest intentions.

He was no longer the dangerous drunk, who once went on stage with an unopened bottle of Jim Beam, and in the middle of 'Bye Bye Blackbird'—the fourth song of the set—put down his guitar and refused to finish the song unless someone brought him a fresh bottle. Instead, he cast himself as the sweet, shaggy man committing only the most forgivable sins—he hit the bottle a little too hard, and talked himself up too much.

He may never have been those other things, but he was in his stories, and his stories were almost all he had left. The woman was gone, and so was his one skill that enabled all the others. He could no longer forgive himself, and no longer improve himself. All that stayed strong was his voice.

Apologies must be made. Not the apologies they give now for their past, but apologies for what they've become. I don't care about my grandfather's violence or my father's whoring. I don't care if their recklessness chopped decades off their wives' old age. I don't care about their guilt. What I can't forgive and I fear I can't escape is the jowly, softhearted pantomimes they've turned themselves into. Is this what happens when women go? The bullet's already been fired and we're left with the shell casings.

Hearing them sing and play, first the carols and then the ballads, broke me up almost as much as my mother's memory. That was how it was supposed to be. There was still a nimbleness to that art, still a ferocity to it. They kept singing, changing back and forth from Irish to hillbilly songs: Ol' Rosin the Beau, Little Maggie, Railroad Boy, Pretty Saro, Lord John, and even as reliable a chestnut as Roll in my Sweet Baby's Arms. For my father, at least, there was no difference between the two styles of music. Us hillbillies had inherited the one worthwhile European tradition. Folk music was our link to the past, before America, before the race as we can imagine it. We alone understood those songs and so we alone were the only part of America that mattered.

People assumed that he married my mother for her accent. It made sense in a way. She was gangly and pale, with bushy eyebrows and enormous hands: nothing like the small, dark women he ran around with. They didn't often fight, but he didn't seem to love her anymore than he loved anyone else. But he did love her accent. It meant she was a witness to all he sang about. That accent validated him, as a singer and as a relic. After people met her, they never doubted my father knew of what he sang. And that's really all he wanted from her or from anyone else.

Those songs were his lexicon, his Bible, and eventually they would become the sum total of his memories. Soon, he wouldn't be able to distinguish his past from those songs, and that was just how he wanted it. He wanted, when people remembered him, to only remember the music. The rest of his life could smear from people's memories like a too wet watercolor, so long as his name brought a song into people's heads.

My father nodded to my grandfather. "You know this one, right? I play it in C." He started pounding the keys, and bobbing his head to the jaunty rhythm. I recognized it before he started singing. Everyone did.

A nation once again,
A nation once again,
O Ireland, long a province be,
A nation once again.

He sang it at my mother's wake, and it was the turning point, at which everyone stopped crying and started singing. Not everyone knew the words at first, but by the end, the entire congregation chanted along to the impossibly optimistic chorus.

People were singing along now, too, although hardly anyone knew what the song meant to him. He saw it as a hillbilly national anthem, albeit one that predated America. It was a rallying cry, and a call home to the Diaspora Appalachians. We would be a nation, forged in as much blood and misery and hope as all other nations in the western world. That was the song's promise, but only my father knew it. The most ridiculous idea of all, and he believed it. All the sincerity he had left was wrapped around that single stupid idea, and I felt a desperate desire to puncture it.

I head myself singing before I knew I was doing it. "Kentucky woman," I sang, much louder than their song. "She gets to know you, she gets to own you."

Jeff put his hand on his my shoulder. "Take it easy, now."

"This man knows it," I said. I pointed to Aunt Marie. "Come on, honey, it's about you. I can't do without, I'm talking about, Kentucky woman."

They had stopped singing now, and were looking at me. My father laughed and hit a few high notes. "Tell me I haven't raised a Neil Diamond fan."

"What?" I said. "I thought I was being patriotic. I'm singing patriotic songs." I looked around.

"We got Betsey Ross over here," Uncle Frankie said. He was laughing, but everyone else looked concerned. "Sing us another, Betsey."

"Let's do Kentucky." I stood up on the piano bench and waved my arms like a conductor. "Kentucky Tucky Bo Bucky, Banana Fanna Fo Fucky, Me My Mo Mucky, Kentucky."

"All right, come on," Jeff said. He stepped towards the piano bench and grabbed my leg. "Play something else, dad."

I threw up my hands, and stepped off the bench, almost tripping on Jeff's foot. "Show's over then, folks. Adieu to you, and you and you and you."

Jeff put his hand on the back of my neck and tried to guide me towards the living room. "Let's talk," he said.

I shook him off me and went into the kitchen instead. "You want a drink?" I hesitated at the whiskey bottle, but then just grabbed a beer. "God knows we got enough."

"Talk to me," he said. "What's the problem?"

I opened the beer. "I was just singing, same as everyone."

He laughed. "Hand me a beer."

I gave him mine and took another for myself.

"It's stupid," he said. "Those songs, you know, it's just pageantry. They do it every year."

"Do they?" I said. "I'm new here."

"When you sing like that." He took a long pull from his beer. "I mean, what's the point, really? What's the point?"

I shrugged. "I'm taking a walk."

"No," he said. "Stay here and talk. It's cold outside."

"It's all right," I said. "A quick walk. Just to move a little bit."

He put his hand on his hip and looked at me. "All right, then, but take a coat." He walked back towards the family, and I went outside.

It was cold, especially with a full beer in my hand, but it was bearable. I sat on the back porch and looked up at the mountains. The miners would take them soon enough. They'd already taken some, and nobody cared enough to stop them. Half of the standing mountains were hollow anyway. These smaller ones survived, but they couldn't last forever. They were the oldest mountains in the world, getting leveled, inch by inch.

I wondered what would happen to my father's romanticism when the miners took the last of them. Once the darker, unexplorable part of the region was exposed, and the hiding places for all the gnomes and giants of his imagination were laid bare, how would he take it? Can a man of his age fall out of love? Maybe the mountains were the one woman he couldn't bear to outlive. Maybe when he saw the last mountain uprooted, he'd crinkle up and die on the spot.

Or maybe it would just make him sing all the louder. He could sing about the past: the dear dead days beyond recall, as the song went, and those memories would only get dearer the worse he remembered them. The easiest songs in the world are those about the past. No one challenges them. No one points to the mountains or the cities and cultures that the mountains spawned and say, 'Look, there's your nation, once again. There's the toothless crowd you're singing love songs too. There.' No one would remember how wrong he was.

From behind me, I heard my uncle Frankie. "Kentucky woman," he sang. "I don't think I have your voice." He sat beside me and laughed his slow raspy laugh. "I got you something." He reached in his jacket pocket and pulled out a fifth of Jim Beam. "Merry Christmas."

"Merry Christmas," I said. "I didn't get you anything."

"Sure you did." He opened up the bottle and took a swig. "You gave me half of this."

I smiled and looked around. "You're not supposed to be drinking, Uncle Frankie." I took the bottle from him and drank.

"I got to hear this from you, too," he said. "You're father's going to skin me alive if he sees me. Terry too." He took the bottle from me, and drank again.

"They know," I said. "So long as it's nothing but drinking, I don't think it'll be too bad."

"That's all it is," he said. He laughed and scratched his forehead. "I liked your songs in there. They're funny."

I took another drink.

"Did I ever tell you this?" he said. "One time, your mother told me I looked just like Cary Grant. She says this on a Monday, and I go through all week, believing it. It goes straight to my head, and I run around, full of myself, talking up every woman I see, getting numbers, dancing, playing the romantic. This lasts all week. Then one week later, I talk to her again, and I realize she was joking with me. I completely took her seriously. But, man, that was your mother. Very funny, you know, and very sly. Not everybody saw that in her, because she was so quiet, but man I'm telling you she was funny." He laughed, gave a faint smile took the bottle and drank.

"Yeah," I said. "Well, what are you going to do?"

He handed me the bottle, stood up, and dusted himself off. "Merry Christmas," he said. "Don't stay out here too long. You'll get sick."

"Merry Christmas," I said. I turned around to watch him leave, and saw my father standing in front of the screen door.

Frankie put his hand on his shoulder as he walked past him. "You sounded good tonight," he said.

My father nodded, walked past him, and sat down beside me. "Hey," he said, "I got you something."

I took a drink from the whiskey.

"Jesus Christ" he said. "That's what I got you. Now it's ruined." He pulled out his bottle of Jim Beam and opened it.

"Merry Christmas," I said.

"Did Frankie give you that?"

"No," I said. "Jeff did."

"Goddamn it," he said. "Son of a bitch hasn't been out of rehab four months, and this is his Christmas gift."

"He's all right."

"I know he's all right," he said. "But how much money are we going to spend on him if this is how he is?" He took a drink. "Jesus, I hit this stuff harder than he does, but he can't handle it. Talk to Terry if you want to know some stories."

"I don't," I said. "Not really."

He took another drink. "This isn't your Christmas gift, by the way. It's just something I thought you'd want."

"It's all right," I said.

He bit his lower lip and played with the top of his bottle. "You were pretty hard on me in there."

I took a drink. "I was just singing," I said. "I'm sorry I interrupted."

He leaned forward and looked up at the mountains. "You still sad?"

"Why feel sad?" I smiled. "I mean, she's up in heaven singing with the angels now, isn't she?"

"You're cute." He took a drink, and, out of habit, offered me the bottle, forgetting I had my own. "It's all right, though, I forgave her."

"You forgave her?"

He smiled. He'd wanted me to react to that, and I cursed myself for falling for it. "That's right," he said. "I forgave her everything."

"That's big of you," I said. "Did you forgive the infidelities? The alcoholism?"

He laughed. "You sound like your sister." He took the bottle back and took a long drink. "It's cold out here," he said when he finished.

"What do you mean, forgive?" He was baiting me, and I hated to act like he expected, but I was curious.

"Forgive," he said. "That's what you do. Forgive."

"Yeah, but what?" I said. "Forgive what?"

He wiped his mouth. "That's all you can do is forgive. Christians got it backwards. They say 'forgive me.' You should say, 'I forgive you of everything you did whether you want me to or not.'"

I coughed and wiped my nose. "This is great. You've turned into the Riddler. What do you mean?"

"If I ask you to forgive me, then I'm presuming. It's not up to me whether you forgive me or not. That's you. All I can do, that I know I can do, is forgive you. That's the one power God can't take from us. I can forgive the whole county if I want."

I took another drink, but the whiskey had stopped tasting good. "So out of curiosity," I said, "do you forgive me?"

"Oh yeah." He patted me on the back. "I forgive everyone here and you have to ask? Of course, I forgive you."

"No," I said. "Fuck that, I forgive you." I raised the bottle. "Try me. Do something lousy, and see if I don't forgive you."

He smiled, took a tentative drink, and put his bottle down in front of me. "We got to get up early tomorrow. Don't stay out here too long."

"If I do," I said, "be sure to forgive me."

He put his hand on the back of my neck and squeezed. The warmth of his hand reminded me how cold I felt. "When someone goes early like this," he said, "especially if it's unexpected and she's close, it's easy to misinterpret it all. What does it mean? It means a lot of things." He scratched his nose and looked down at his knees. "But there's something you should take from it, and I know you've heard it before, but it's important, as far as it goes."

"All right." I took another drink. I didn't want it anymore, but I didn't want to flinch in front of him.

He brought his hand up to his face and then back down again. "It's important that you don't smoke," he said. "Your mother smoked a lot and it weakens your heart, your lungs, everything. This never would've happened if she didn't smoke."

"Don't smoke?" I gave him a lopsided smile. "That's all right, I don't smoke."

"Good," he said. "I smoke a little, but I never got addicted. Your mom got hooked so bad, I swear she was breathing as much smoke as air. She rolled her own half the time. Said she couldn't taste it otherwise."

"I don't smoke," I said. "Not even a little."

"Well all right," he said. "Then I guess you're safe." He looked around behind him, and then up to the sky. "Christmas tomorrow," he said. "I'm getting you up early." He smiled, saluted, and then turned around and went inside.

I stood up and then sat back down, unsure if I wanted to walk the neighborhood, or fall asleep. Now there were two heavily dented whiskey bottles in front of me, neither of which I wanted anything to do with. Still, just to see if I could, I took two sips of each, held them in my mouth and let them linger in the back of my throat before swallowing. It was going to hurt tomorrow, but that was tomorrow.

I was safe. Don't smoke and you'll be safe. That was the moral of my mother's life, according to the one adult who kind of loved her. At least, there was a moral and a comforting one, too. He'd given her that and it was better than nothing. Better for the lines to be badly drawn than there be no lines at all.

I rapped my knuckles against the porch and began repeating my mother's full name. "Cathleen Margaret Donohue Clay." It had a nice rhythm, spoken aloud like that. I leaned into the words, landing on each of the syllables equally. "Cath leen mar ga ret don o hue clay. Cath leen mar ga ret don o hue clay." I repeated it, first aloud, then silently, until I began hearing it in my head without moving my mouth.

In the weeks after the stroke, I would stay awake until the early morning, silently mouthing her name in what I knew was a repetition, but felt different and more painful each time. It wasn't like that anymore. Her names were just words and, stretched out and repeated like that, just syllables, to be arranged and rearranged in any way I saw fit.

I'd outlived one woman and there would be others. Maybe I'd already started to lose a little liveliness myself, and maybe that was what stopped the pain. If so, it was well worth it. I put my hands together and improvised a prayer:

Lord, do what you will with my reputation, my memories, my judgment, and my intentions. Cast me off into obscurity, eons away from anyone who might know me let alone love me. Deny me heaven and deny me life. But, O Lord, protect me from pain. I can take anything but pain.

I picked up the bottles and screwed their caps on. There was plenty left for Christmas, and, if I hid one from my family, then it may last until New Year's.

The lights in the house were off. No one else was going to check on me, and there was no use staying cold. Next year, the memory would be even smaller. I may never be able to make myself believe I sprang fully formed, without the same cord attached back to her womb that the rest of the world has, but it would be easier next year. For now, all there was to do was go inside, lie down someplace warm and wait for Christmas.

Mikey Delgado

Secure

Today I'm as fragile as the sky. The newspaper says that prisoner planes are busy in the European skies and I put the paper down. Reading about those planes has made me hot. I put too many t-shirts on this morning. I've done so much wrong in my time that it can only be a matter of time before they come for me and it's making me sweat when I read about people being arrested and flown to places to be tortured. The thought of having someone torture you just to see what it is that you are thinking makes me sweat. I said as much to Straw. I told him that. You know what the crazy bastard said to me? He said that you can't beat a bit of red in photographs!

"What photographs?"

"These."

And he put three photographs down on the table. He's

torn them from some magazine or other. It's just like him to tear them out rather than cut them out. I said that to him. I said why do you tear them out? I did. I asked him that. I said *you're such an impatient bastard, why didn't you cut them out and make them nice neat rectangles?* He said *all this,* and he pointed to the ragged bits of magazine around the edge of the photographs, *all this gives a context that isn't available to us otherwise.* And around the edges of these photographs there are bits of stories and exhortations and advertisements from the magazine he's ripped the pictures out of.

"Look at this for instance," he says, and he shows me the edge of one photograph and there's part of a little column advert which says

Do you need money?
Yes?
Your worries are over, just…

Straw is writing away in his notebook. I asked him what he's writing and he says he's writing down proof. He says he's writing about how taking part in the world is a game and that it has to be played. It's all been decided long ago. He says that things have to be remembered and things have to be forgotten and that this remembering and forgetting is automatic in healthy people.

"That's all mental health is," he says.

He's writing in his notebook that he knows the rules of remembering and forgetting but that he just can't do it properly and so he just looks foolish playing it. He says it's for Doctor Wilson, this writing.

"Wilson wants me out of here. I know he does. He thinks I could take it out there. But I'm not fit. What could I do out in the world but crumble? This place isn't so much better but I know what happens. I remember and forget better in here too. He thinks I'd survive out there but I won't, I know I won't"

I don't like it when Straw talks like this. He wants to stay ill. That's what I tell him. I tell him he's afraid of getting better. He tells me he's the sanest person he knows. He says that Wilson is one of the craziest. *But having said that,* he says, *there's not much in it anyway. For any of us.*

"How do you like the photographs?" he asks.

I can hardly bear to look at them. I'm so fragile today that anything that fascinates Straw is probably going to terrify me but I don't say that. I change the subject. I tell him that I just don't like Doctor Wilson. I tell him that in my opinion it's not about sane or crazy, it's about nice or not nice and I don't think Wilson's nice.

"People like that shouldn't have any power over the lives of other people. They don't know what it is to be human. They only know what it is to be them," I say.

Straw gathers the three photographs from the table. He rips two of them into shreds and puts the other one back onto the table.

"I'll just keep this one," he says. "The red in this is the

best. If you have three photographs you like you should tear two of them up. You know Wilson's trouble? When you watch people all day you realise that someone is watching you too."

He looks at me. "But you know that," he says.

Doctor Wilson comes and sits alongside us. "Enjoying a nice cup of tea, chaps?" he asks.

Straw closes his notebook and pushes his cup away.

"It's horrible tea here."

"Why drink it then?" asks Wilson.

"Because it's what they give us," says Straw.

I can smell the antiseptic hand-wash that Wilson uses after he's handled files. I wonder if he's been looking at mine.

Wilson talks about the trees...the ones over there, beyond the window...he says that he hadn't realised (jesus!) how many greens there are in them. I try to not let it show anywhere on my face that I'm thinking how incredible it is that he should say that. This is a man who looks for clues as to what ails us. He spends his life doing that. He's the senior man here. When I first came here they told me that Wilson is good at this job, very good, so it seemed odd to me that he should have said that. It seemed odd that he could have sat here and drunk so much coffee every morning break and every afternoon break, facing those trees over there, and it had only just occurred to him that a line of trees can have so many greens in it.

Wilson turns and looks at me in that way that I don't like. He looks at me and waits just that bit too long before he says anything. It always feels as if he's already listening to me before I've even said anything out loud, as if he's already got hold of me like some shell and has me held up to his ear. He catches me off guard when he says, "Do you know what I'm thinking?" because that is exactly what I'm thinking. I'm thinking *does he know what I'm thinking?*

"I'm thinking," he says "that you and I will go to the ground floor and you can bring your camera and take photographs. You take some interesting shots I hear. They tell me that it's your hobby. I'd like to see what it is that you see down there that seems important enough to you to document."

They told me when I first came here that Wilson always wants to take you down there, down to the ground floor, to see how you do, but I never want to go there. I know I'll feel ill there. I'll get dizzy. I won't like the air. I'll worry about the time. Or I'll worry about whether it's dark outside yet. I'll be thinking that when I finally get out of there everyone in the rest of the world will be gone and the streets outside will be as empty as some of the corridors we see on the monitors in here late in the evening. There are no clocks down there. They don't want you to worry about what time it is. There are no windows. They don't want you to think that it's time to be going. They don't want you to think of a view you know of, a place where at the time the clock may show there will be lights going on in houses across the fields from where you could be standing if you weren't here.

They don't want you to know how much of the day has been lost.

They want you to think that all there is in the world are shops and cafés and escalators and crowds and cameras and plastic cards and coins and impulses and the smells of people and the smells of scents and chemists and papers and food. But there's anxiety down there, I know there is, and in enclosed spaces like that it's infectious. And there is some portion of people down there with no other thought than to do what they are encouraged to do and some portion of people with no other thought than to steal. And there are one or two people in every corridor ready to explode. And these one or two will have no idea that they are the ones who are dangerous today, and they will want to explode next to me. They will want to take their faulty remembering and forgetting out on me and I won't know what to do.

"What do you think of that idea?" asks Wilson, and I don't know if he means what do I think about his suggestion or what do I think about what his suggestion has made me think.

I wish he'd said *why are you here?* instead. I could have said then that I was sent here and that I didn't have any choice. They don't give you any choice. Some guy with a few O-levels looks at the paper in front of him and sends you here and that's it. But Doctor Wilson knows that and he doesn't care about that. Wilson doesn't like whingers.

So I don't say to him that I don't know anything much about photography. I don't. You probably know more than I do. All I know is what looks mysterious to me and I know what makes me agitated and I know what that French guy said about a photograph being invisible. But that's it. Marsham, the guy who ran away on his very first day here, after the breakfast break, seemed to have a point. He said that morning, with a mouthful of croissant, that a photograph is a miniscule section of the world and that's all. But Doctor Wilson thinks that the pictures we take are all that's important. He thinks they tell him all he needs to know. At least I see what Straw means by context. Wilson doesn't. But he doesn't have to. It's not his job to consider that.

Wilson gets up. He looks at Straw. "I'm seeing you later, aren't I?" he asks.

"The letter from the office says three o'clock," says Straw. I can feel that Straw feels like a child who wants to beg *Mummy, no, please, no.*

Wilson looks at him in something like the same way that he looks at me. He looks at him as if he's looking at his face so he can describe it later in very great detail, even how much it may measure from hairline to chin, from ear to ear.

Doctor Wilson points to the table. "Bring that photo you've torn out of whatever it is you've torn it out of. We can talk about it."

He says that he'll be back soon to take me downstairs. I feel sick. I feel as old as a chair and I feel like a child who's been told of a new punishment. I pick up the photograph that Straw wants me to look at. I want to be in it, between the camera and the furthermost background, so I can take my mind off how fearful I am. The sky is so white today, like the surface on the inside of an eggshell, that you can't help worrying about what is really on the other side of it.

Straw is excited. He likes it that I'm looking at the photograph. He thinks I'm showing an interest in something that interests him about this world.

"Look at the red," he says. I think his voice is quivering. "See what a difference it makes."

He's right. It does. The photograph becomes invisible. You enter it, and in it their hands claw the sky and their heads wear red haloes against the sand. Their stilled eyes are staring at the blue sector of the sky beyond the high clouds under which they lay. In the dust of a landscape like this memory grows like knotweed. I look at their hands, their stiffened open fists surrendering. If you wanted to, after you put Straw's photograph down, you could remember their hands as babies' hands, reaching for assurance; delicate, tiny baby fingers curled around the finger of a man. If remembering and forgetting were done differently their heads might not have red haloes against the sand. They might still be living. They might instead be sipping coffee from cups as small as thimbles, and on the table there could be a plant with red flowers, and mothers holding babies in their arms, wanting for nothing.

Wilson has steel tips on his heels. I can hear him coming. Straw takes the ragged paper with the photograph on. As he folds it I catch a glimpse of the word *orgasm* in a sentence under the picture of the dead Afghans.

"Listen to those shoes," says Straw. "Even from that you can hear why they call him doctor. The clinical bastard. He even sounds surgical, the way he walks."

Wilson has my jacket. He hands it to me and I put it on as we leave the room which faces that line of trees. I follow him to the stairs that lead down to the ground floor. The yellow fluorescence of his own jacket and the glare of the ceiling lights colliding with the reflective strip across the back of it which says *Security* makes me feel more ill. The steel tips on his shoes sound urgent against the empty stairs.

Mikey Delgado

Hodgepewter and Pantani go undercover at the Glastonbury festival

When Detective Sergeant Mario Hodgepewter said to Detective Constable Marco Pantani that he adored Glastonbury he made it clear to Pantani that he was using the word *adore* in an *ultra-imaginative* way. He said that when he conjured up a vision, for instance, of an Egyptian Pharaoh with people prostrating themselves before him, and he compared that image to a series of mental pictures of Glastonbury, and then introduced the word *adore* into his mindscape there was a resonance, as if the link should be at least considered for meaning.

"Of course the meaning is ultimately completely removed from *adore*. It is the remotest word from any explanation of what I am attempting to convey to you...except for all the other words that exist in our language. Thus it is the closest word that I can use to describe how I love this place," he said.

Pantani, tripping as he is on Welsh mushrooms, sees what Hodgepewter is getting at. He feels that *worship* rather than *adore* might be better in the case of the Pharaoh, and *fear* might be better still but, since he is more anxious that Hodgepewter shouldn't bother himself explaining exactly what he means by *love* in this context, he keeps his reservations to himself. Pantani wants to stay on his buzz.

"Oh yes Mario," he quickly agrees. "It all depends on our instant analysis of the word and its surrounding statement."

"Exactly, Marco," says Hodgepewter. "We must deduce as best we can from the context."

Johnny Fandango the fire-eater is swallowing flaming torches around the campfire. He watches in fascination as the shadows of the flames and their yellow light play across Hodgepewter's and Pantani's narrowed eyes. Before Hodgepewter can start on an explanation of exactly what he means by *exactly* Johnny Fandango speaks.

"So I take it" says Johnny, addressing Hodgepewter and Pantani, "from the brand new trainers you two are wearing, and your impeccably combed and parted hair, that you are both undercover police officers. I further take it that luckily, given the nature of your assignment, you enjoy taking drugs both recreationally and as a long-term lifestyle choice. I take it further still that you are both in the fortunate position of being agents of the state's monopoly power to impound certain drugs which the state has deemed it unseemly for its subjects to have access to. It seems, from the interesting little collection of samples that you have in front of you, that you have availed yourself of the opportunity to use your warrant cards to intercept many of the youth at this get-together and confiscate their supplies in order to smoke or swallow them yourselves."

"My word! Got it one Johnny," said Hodgepewter. "There's a job for you in criminal investigations if you ever decide that fire-swallowing isn't the life for you. That's quite remarkable."

"Simple enough," says Johnny. "One learns to watch the audience when one is fire-eating. The communion with the audience is very close to the link established in the sex act when a participant is absent from their eyes and the other partner is drawn to that fascinating sight of the lover being absent. So one watches closely. One takes every opportunity to observe without being observed."

"Indeed one does," says Hodgepewter. "I had noticed that you are rather like a cobra charmer, Mr Fandango. You hold the audience such that, as you have hinted, you hypnotise them into a kind of mindless collective. Marco here and myself use a similar technique in our interrogations. We act out a drama we have devised and I have to say it's most effective. Of course the writing seems derivative once you are aware it is scripted drama and not a spontaneous performance that one is watching, but nevertheless in a police interview room to have striven each time for the flawless performance is quite an exhilarating feeling. If I may nod to Huxley's epigraph while making it absolutely clear that the link to it is nevertheless extremely casual, I should say that one never leaves the room the same man as one enters it."

Pantani calculates that the hallucinogens in the mushrooms he has ingested are nearing their maximum activity. He is enjoying watching the tent nearest them morph into a bicycle made for two. Nevertheless he feels compelled to add to the conversation before Hodgepewter has a chance to begin explaining the intricacies of the word *casual*.

"It's called *the Hodgepewter method*," explains Pantani. "We achieve remarkable results but it is, I don't mind saying, a lonely kind of acting."

"I can see that it would be," says Johnny Fandango. He twiddles with both ends of his luxurious moustache. "But it is art and art is a solitary pursuit in the area in which the two of you and I work."

Johnny takes a swig of paraffin and sprays it with some force from his mouth onto a burning torch. He sends a flame fifteen feet to where a garrulous youth is advertising his business with the shouted refrain that he has more drugs to sell than *Boots*. Hodgepewter makes a mental note to bust the lad later and test his claim that the black hash he is selling is the best this side of the Rif mountains.

"When Rationalism is swept away and snooker is televised without cease" continues Johnny, "the sole opposition to snooker in the ratings war will be the art and trickery of encouraging a man to believe he is guilty of a crime that he didn't commit. There will be superstars. You may feel that you are ploughers of a lonely furrow now but, never fear, you will be remembered as artists, laying a path for the television stars of tomorrow."

Hodgepewter nods sagely. Pantani confesses that he himself is a great fan of the work of Busby Berkeley. He says that he would like to turn the interrogation sessions into musicals with intricately achieved dance sequences.

"Particularly when interrogating murderers, god-botherers, and kiddy-fiddlers," he says.

"We must be patient, Marco" says Hodgepewter. "We may yet see it in our lifetime. The Chief Commissioner wasn't absolutely opposed to the idea of musical interrogations when I raised the possibility with him. But nothing can happen before its time."

Pantani fears that he is now too intoxicated to distract Hodgepewter from enlarging on his theories about the possible meanings of *time*. Luckily, beside them, a shape emerges from underneath a blanket. Chief Superintendent Felicity Purges is groggy, only now coming round from an episode of insensibility caused by an extremely intense rush to the brain of psilocybin compounds.

"Christ," she dribbles.

"These mushrooms were grown above fifteen hundred feet, ma'am," explains Pantani. "They are from the Rhondda Valley. They are rather vigorous."

"You're telling me," says Felicity Purges.

Her eyes are like two delicate saucers, each with a pale blue island and a black dot at their centre.

"I'm getting too old for this," she says.

Hodgepewter wonders whether it is the inhalation of the fumes of a most agreeable Nepalese temple ball that is making him feel so fondly towards Felicity. She is someone's daughter, a policewoman, undercover, and, Hodgepewter fears, out of her depth. Felicity Purges would probably agree with the latter assessment. She has voluntarily changed the nature of her consciousness and she is rather regretting the sudden incapacity of her brain's reducing filter. On the periphery of her vision there is a panther with yellow eyes and a red tongue, prowling, waiting for her to pass out. This hallucinating business is OK for five minutes or so, she thinks. All the pretty colours and the million thoughts a second are rather a novelty, but she hates that long slow comedown and the feeling between her legs that she can do nothing about in front of Hodgepewter and Pantani. The wanting to writhe naked on dew-soaked grass and rub herself raw won't let her alone. And even the little moments of clarity which have led her to keep a notebook in which she notes down her thoughts and registers her surprise at the nuggets of wisdom which surface from the colours, even these moments are impossible to recapture and examine after the affects have worn off. With eyes whose sockets feel like they are stuffed with cotton wool and powdered glass, she stares at the words she has written and wonders what they mean…what on earth could Hodgepewter have meant…*so much depends, ma'am, upon a red wheelbarrow glazed with rainwater…*?

Pantani doesn't care. He is enjoying the buzz. He has noticed he can see through the clothes of every woman wearing yellow.

Hodgepewter is eating his dinner by firelight. It is spaghetti. The spaghetti is squirming like a pit of snakes.

Johnny Fandango swallows a burning bush.

Bryan Edenfield

Laser God

I got into a theological debate with the cashier at a gas station convenient store (as I often do) and he was telling me how he was atheist, and how he thought all those nut cases that believed in god were just kidding themselves, and wasting their time. We got into this discussion because I asked him why the bean burritos were so over priced. I asked him, I said, "Hey, boyo, why these bean burritos so over priced? I am outraged!"

He then looked at me and shrugged passively. "It's not my fault. Don't blame me."

I became angry at him for this. Since he and I were the only two people in the store, I really had no other choice but to blame him. I of course can't blame myself, because I'm never wrong and never do anything that isn't good and pure and perfect. And I must blame someone, because everything is always someone else's fault, and that fault needs to be handed out right away.

So I handed out the fault to him, because he was the only other person there. It was quite late at night, and the gas station was a pretty out of the way one. The convenient store that went hand in hand with the gas station wasn't actually very convenient, but I suppose calling it an inconvenient store wouldn't help business too much.

Now, you're probably wondering, what brought me way out to this inconvenient gas station in the middle of the night. Well, that's a long and interesting story that involves dazzling adventures with a sexy anthropologist named Bambi, horrifying terror that involves evil killer dwarfs, and humorous sexual escapades with the entire female cast of Friends. I'm not going to tell you about this though. Instead, I'm going to tell you about the boring theological debate I got into with the snot nosed elitist atheist cashier.

So there I was, and the cashier's words were ringing in my brilliant head. "Don't blame me." I exploded. This hurt, but not as much as one may think.

"What do you mean, don't blame you? There's no one else in this fucking store!" I screamed like a gypsy having an orgasm. "I have to blame someone, and you're the only one here! Unless you suggest I blame God. Who do you want me to blame, God? Do you want me to blame fucking God? How about these potato chips! Shall I blame them!!!"

"I don't believe in god, " the cashier said. I looked at his name tag. His name was Chris. It figured. All people named Chris are atheists.

I shook my head at this, "What the fuck do I care?"

"I'm an atheist, I don't believe in god. I think it's ludicrous. Some all powerful being up in imaginary land controlling our faith. It's all a bunch of bull. There's absolutely nothing pointing to the existence of god. The whole idea is just dumb. People who believe in god are dumb. Any reasonable person, if they think about it, will come to the conclusion that there is no, never was, and never can be, a god. It's impossible."

This annoyed me. Not because I believe in God, because, for all practical purposes, I don't. I consider myself an agnostic. It annoyed me because I wanted to buy my bean burrito, and he was blabbin' on about some stupid god he didn't believe in. He kept blabbing.

"I mean, look at the world around you. There are laws. There aren't angels flying around, touchin' people. Della Reese isn't goin' around saving people and pulling people out of wells. And, you notice it's only nutcases in third world countries that see Jesus in there soup. And really, soup is like clouds, you can see anything you want to see. It's all in the mind. It's all a psychological crutch. Opium for the masses, as Lenin said."

This really made me mad. The reasons why go on and on.

And he continued. "There are no miracles. Have you ever seen a miracle? I sure haven't. And when strange things happen, there's always a scientific explanation. Or it's just a coincidence. There are no miracles, there is no god. The world is governed and controlled by scientific laws and patterns. It's all patterns. This has been proven. God hasn't been proven. Scientist's aren't looking in telescopes and looking into space and saying, 'Hey look, there's God right next to Jupiter. He's waving at me. Wave back, Charly. Man, that guy's got some nice teeth. Who ya think does his dental work?' They ain't seein' that when they look up into space, no siree. They see planets, and asteroids, and science. They see science. All this religion stuff, it's just for the weak. It's for the weak and the stupid."

I was exhausted at this point. I had dropped my bean burrito, and repeatedly jumped on it out of frustration. I had cracked the tile floor. My feet were actually bleeding. They didn't hurt though. I was too exhausted to feel pain.

"So," Chris said, "what do you think?"

I looked up and made that face like Malcolm McDowell in A Clockwork Orange. You know, the milk drinkin' face. I calmed myself down, and prepared to speak.

"Well, dude, what do you think?"

"It seems to me," I began slowly, "that your science is just as much of a joke as religion. It seems to me that you're just like all those Bible lovers knocking at my door trying to sell me vacuum cleaners. It seems to me you're as wrapped up in all this as a person who believes in God. So really, what's the point either way?"

I angered Chris with this. He gave me a look that I can't describe by comparing it to a movie. Well, maybe I can. Remember the look the T-Rex made before he ate the lawyer in Jurassic Park? It's not that look, but my dog sometimes makes that look, and it's the funniest thing.

"What do you mean? You're completely wrong. I can't express how wrong you are! Science isn't the same joke as religion. Science has proof to back it up! Proof! Religion ain't got no proof. What does religion have? Some 2000 year old dead dudes who talk vaguely about seeing god, and they were probably all on drugs. Drug use has been around along time. How is it we take seeing god seriously, but not the delusions of someone who drops acid! It's preposterous! Fucking absurd! Science has proof. Religion has delusions."

"How do you know you aren't having a delusion right now?" I asked.

"'Cause I ain't on no fucking drugs."

"Yes, but it's late. You're working the late shift, I'm sure you're a bit tired. Maybe you've fallen asleep. Maybe this is all a dream. I mean, what is proof? What are facts? They're just delusions shared by massive amounts of people. Or better yet, they're delusions shared by a bunch of intellectuals who have proclaimed themselves to be the creators of truth. There's no difference between this and religion. You have those in religion who proclaim what they experience is the TRUTH and you have those in science who proclaim that what they experience is the TRUTH. And science is such a baby. Science could prove the existence of

God if it really wanted to. Science could prove anything. Science could prove the existence of unicorns if it wanted to. You have the atom for example. Who the hell's seen an atom? No one. Not even scientists. If I'm not mistaking, no stupid telescope can see an atom. The science type guys, they're shootin' lasers or something, and they see the laser beam, it's bouncin' off of somethin', or it's reflectin' off of somethin', or it's slowin' down because of somethin', and they're sayin' ,' Woa, that laser hit something! What do you think it is, Larry?' 'I think we've just discovered the smallest particle of life, Kent. We'll call it an atom.' 'Yes, an atom. We've just discovered an atom. We can't see it, but we know it's there because a laser beam is hittin' it!' The scientists could have just as easily have said, 'Oh my, the laser beam is hittin' somethin'! It must be God! Oh no, we've discovered God, and he's tiny, but he's everywhere!' 'Turn off the laser, Larry, you're shootin' God! You're shootin' God with a laser beam! You're gonna piss him off, Larry!'" At this point, I began to get a little carried away, and my imagination took over.

"'Stop shootin' God with a laser! He's gonna smite us!!' And then God will come and manifest himself, and be like, 'STOP SHOOTING ME WITH THE LASER, THAT REALLY TICKLES. AND NOT IN THE GOOD WAY, IN THE BAD ANNOYING WAY. DON'T MAKE ME GET VENGEFUL ON YOU.' And then God will take the scientist that shot him with a laser, and the scientist will be like, 'Are you going to kill me?' and God will say, 'NO LARRY, I WON'T, I WILL CAUSE AN ACCIDENT TO HAPPEN TO YOU THAT WILL HAVE HORRIBLE, IRONIC RESULTS. FOR EXAMPLE, IF YOU ARE A

HOMOPHOBE, YOU'RE WIFE WILL GIVE BIRTH TO A GAY SON. OR, IF YOU ARE A DOCTER, I WILL GIVE YOU A DISEASE MEDICAL SCIENCE CAN'T CURE. OR, IF YOU ARE A RACIST, I WILL CAUSE YOU TO BE IN A HORRIBLE CAR ACCIDENT THAT WILL TURN YOU INTO A BLACK PERSON, FOR SOME REASON.' So then, all these scientists will start being nice to God, and they'll offer him donuts and candy. But there'll be these rebel scientists that figure they can destroy God by shooting him with lasers. So they'll all get laser guns and run around shootin' God with lasers, and Nietzsche will come running out screaming, 'Stop it, you're killing God!' but they'll keep doing it, and they'll kill God, and Nietzsche will say, 'Well, there, you've gone and done it. You've killed God. God is dead. Are you happy.' And he'll walk away, and then everybody will see this guy walking on a tight rope, and they'll all look at him and smile and say, 'Hey look, that guy's walking on a tight rope.' And everyone will be very impressed, and then they'll all die." I took a breath. "Can I have my bean burrito now?"

"That'll be $3.99."

"Horribly overpriced," I said, paying the man, and going back outside to continue my exciting intergalactic adventures.

Timothy Gager

Flying to Los Angeles

I was off to Los Angeles to see my sister and also some gal that drinks too much and sleeps around. I'm going to see that one first, rather than my sister who doesn't even know I'm coming. The girl, my love interest, met me at the airport and due to my fear of flying I was already intoxicated and dangerously close to an overdose of airsickness pills. Too much of these both and I knew I was going to be of no use to her. She'd wanted to go out, already had a babysitter, but I'd just rather pass out at her place in Burbank. "You're useless," she verified. "And I can't even hang tomorrow, have to work. Emergency. Do you think you can just hang out until I get back without getting in any trouble?"

"Yeah."

"I need to get a babysitter also. The one I have tonight can't help me out tomorrow morning. She can come back at night though. We'll go do something"

"I can watch the kids during the day," I offered.

"You sure…"

"Yeah. Had two of my own. I'm a pro."

She had two kids ages five and six months, but was only in her early twenties. She had a really good job and was doing well providing as a single mom. My own children were much older so I've pretty much handled anything these two could dish out. I've done it all before, knew schedules, understood naps and could whip up some fish sticks and Cheerios with the best of them. Mya would leave at seven AM, by back by five or six then we could get going, go out and do something fun. It was all OK with me, but as soon as I got back to her place, I passed out and the alarm rang.

"Kids should be up soon."

"Uhhhh," I groaned.

"You're going to be fine today, aren't' you?"

"Yeah, " I said.

"You're not doing to beat or kill them?"

"Haven't met them yet. No guarantees," I managed a phony laugh so that she wouldn't think I was being serious.

"OK," she said.

"OK," I added and she was gone to the office.

It always happens early in the morning that the second you shut your eyes to go back to sleep, either the snooze alarm goes off, some woman kicks you, or some other asshole rings the phone. It's just what life is, unless you have a gold pass from God, you aren't allowed you to sleep well. Today it was Mya's oldest, running into the bed to see his mom, seeing me instead and screaming.

"Don't worry, I'm a friend of your mom. Don't cry, I'll get you breakfast."

"Waffles," he sniffed.

"Yeah, I promise." The baby was still asleep until the time I found the house to be waffle-less and now I had two pissed off kids. One crying because I'd broken a promise and the other awake but still tired, with of a sack of shit for a diaper. "Yeah, babygirl, I'll change you, " I said to her. She looked like Mya. "Hey you!" I called to the brother, "What's your sister's name and as long as I'm at it, what's yours?"

"I'm Colin and that's Caitlin. We call her Kate." Strange, I thought. Two Irish names for the Asian mother. She must not have named them, I concluded.

"She's hungry," Colin said. At least he wasn't crying anymore, he was in helper mode. I could tell that he cared for his sister and the waffle tragedy was all but put aside. A good kid. My own would have throttled the sister silly when I wasn't looking. 7:19, so far, so good and everything was easy. Her next nap would be around lunch and I was confident I could make it to that milestone, even if there was nothing to eat in the house. I had opened some cabinets and found vodka, gin, rum and a case of red wine. There was some cereal there, Cocoa Sweeties, but not much else. Maybe we could all go to the store and stock the house. Maybe I could be the responsible one for once. Maybe, I'll hit the vodka during Kate's nap. Regardless of the plans in my head, they both had Cocoa Sweeties without milk and I fixed Kate a bottle of water for TV time. It felt all so familiar, watching these kids, relying on my past experiences. Even in the past, no matter how bad it got my wife and I would have had food available. When we divorced I would go with minimal supplies similar to what was at Mya's place. It was a time that my own kids were in their teens and didn't need or want anything from me. They would grow up and be fine without much effort from me. At least they still knew their Daddy, unlike Mya's children whose own father had little involvement. Or so I thought. Based on her children's reactions I assumed they had met some similar men to myself whether they realized the pattern or not. They may have been similar but not as good as me, the about to be anointed hero, ready to order a Dominos Pizza for lunch. I figured this to be my best option, since I had no idea where a store might be located in Mya's neighborhood. Colin started jumping around when I told him of the lunch plans and then turned to his sister who was perched on my shoulder and said in his tiniest baby voice, "We're having pizza for lunch." Kate, excited by the attention, kicked her legs into my balls.

"She likes pizza," Colin said to me still in his Kate-talk. "When's it going to get here?" It took me a few seconds to catch my breath.

"Maybe thirty minutes. I have to cook it."

"Is that fast?"

"Yeah about as long as…" I looked at the TV. "Spongebob. When Spongebob is finished the pizza should be here."

The show ended and the pizza was late. "I'm hungry," Colin said. I reassured him that it would be here very soon. The phone rang. It was Mya. "How's it going?"

"Good. The kids love me. I ordered a pizza."

"You are good. I may have to fire the baby-sitter."

"No problem. I'll just hang here, perhaps drink some of your booze." Kate was tired, starting to get fussy.

"Kate's tired," Mya added. "I got plenty of…"

"Yeah, I noticed. That's about all that you got here."

"I meant to shop. Thanks for picking up the pizza, Matt."

"Welcome."

"And by the way, Kevin may be…oh shit the boss is here. Got to run sweetie."

"Kevin? What time are you…?" It was too late. She had hung up, but Colin standing right next to me. He was crawling up my ass waiting for me to finish on the telephone. "When's the pizza coming?" There was a knock on the door and as a turned to get it I almost tripped on Colin.

"Jesus, it's here!" I snapped, regaining my footing. I opened the door and saw a larger version of Colin, covered in tattoos standing at the door. I focused on his left arm, covered in spider-web ink, an octopus, dark veined plants, a tower with the word Mya engraved inside and something else with the word "Mom."

"Who are you?" he asked gruffly. Normally I'd answer that with my pat, "Who the hell are you?" but because I was in a strange environment and the pure size of this guy, having my ass kicked was not on the lunch schedule. Colin sprinted by, yelling, "Daaaad!" I turned to the big man, placed Kate in his arms and said, "I'm Matt. The baby-sitter."

"He's a friend of Mom," Colin stated.

"Yeah, right," he snarled. "Kevin." I stuck out my hand to shake his, but he just looked at it. "I don't like shaking hands. I think it's stupid."

"Umm OK."

"I don't know why people do it at all with all the germs and shit. Anyway don't sweat the fact I'm here. I'm done with that bitch. Found her with someone else and that was it." His statement got me thinking of why relationships don't work and why Mya could have cheated. Perhaps there was not enough anti-bacterial soap in the house for him to scrub himself off after sex.

"You want some pizza, Dad?" Colin asked, changing the subject.

"Sure squirt. I'll take a slab."

"It's not here yet," I cut into their conversation and was met with an immediate look of contempt.

"Not here yet? It's right around the corner. Best pizza in Los Angeles."

The door was still open and the pizza boy was looking in. "Dominos," he shouted. "Shitty pizza," Kevin stated directly to the teen that was not expecting to be treated in this manner. "$13.47," the teen added quietly. I reached into my wallet and pulled out a twenty. "I'll pay for my own kids," Kevin snapped. "Just give me a ten." Somehow the math seemed a little off unless his kids were worth only $3.47, not including the tip. Funny that Kevin was providing for his kids, yet I was still paying for the pie. He handed the delivery boy my ten and another five. "Got an extra buck for the tip?" Kevin asked. I gave pizza boy another single, while Kevin brought the pizza to the table. "Mya should have told you about Jefe's around the corner."

"I didn't know about Jefe's. I just got in last night...I mean early this morning. We hardly..."

"Last night? This morning? Save it for someone who gives a shit," Kevin interrupted. The phone rang and Kevin snapped it up. "Hello. Oh hi honey," he said sarcastically. "Yeah I'm still here. Still here!" he loudly laughed. "You want to speak with Matt? He's still here too. Yeah, well that fine with me and I DO have to be such an asshole, darling!" He flipped me the phone and said to me in the same sarcastic tone of voice, "Honey, it's for you."

"He'll leave soon," was the first thing out of Mya's mouth.

"It's fine, whatever," I said, not really convincing her.

"Sorry. This must be a crappy way to start a vacation. I'll try to make it up to you."

"Sounds good. What time are you coming home?" I asked. Kevin looked over, "What time are you coming home" he mimicked, almost in Colin's baby talk voice.

"Maybe five, maybe six. Depends on what time I got out of here as well as the traffic. I'll try to get there as soon as I can."

I hung up and Kevin was standing right next to me. Like father like son I thought. "I'm not planning on leaving anytime soon," he said to me. "I don't trust strangers around my kids. You understand, don't you?" While I was on the phone he had put Kate down for a nap. "Want a beer?" he asked. Looked like an afternoon of drinking beer with Kevin was set if I could tolerate it.

We would all sit on the stained sofa and watch TV for a few hours. Perhaps after a few drinks, I'd think of him as a decent guy. Beer drinking often will do that. "Most guys take off after getting a look at me," Kevin said. "Not that I care, but it's kind of amusing chasing some of them off. Thing is that I really don't care, about her, but I do about my kids. I think Mya's a train wreck."

"She said that you hardly came by," I stated, almost regretting the words as they fell out of my mouth.

"Of course she said that. Would you have come by if you knew I was going to be here?" I didn't answer. "I thought that to be the case," he laughed. He was a real charmer.

I was starting to feel a slight buzz from the beer, and Kevin just kept talking. It was easy just to listen at this point. He talked about the tightness of his family and how Mya hated hers. He talked about how he couldn't work all the time and how difficult it was for him to afford his rent on what he made. He talked about his drinking and the fights he and Mya used to have. He talked a lot about the children, Colin and Kate. Kate was now awake, lying on a blanket and batting at a toy. He talked and drank until it was close to five PM. The kids were good, they seemed to handle it all in stride, Colin with his cartoons and Kate being carried around by Kevin most of the time. At this time a young woman came in. It was Kelly, the babysitter. She got as far as the doorway as Kevin took out his wallet, put money in her hand, and gave her a long full-lipped kiss. "See you in a bit," he said. I sat, stoned, still on the sofa as she turned, and was gone. I had become the unwilling participant of a Jerry Springer show. It had been an odd day.

Mya was the next to enter the Springer studio. She took one look at Kevin and me on the sofa, beer in my hand and stopped dead in her tracks. I was glad she didn't attack either of us, which is what would have happened if we lived in TV Land. "God. Fucking men!" she exclaimed, looking at me. "This is great. Maybe it would have been better if he had chased you out." Kevin was equally cold, but responded to her. "Hell, he wouldn't go, but I will right now. Got some plans, perhaps dinner and dancing with Kelly. She's free tonight, I heard."

"What??"

"Yeah, I heard it directly from her. She was here. Don't worry she said she'd be back in the morning," he smiled. "Remember, I always win. Later dude."

Mya began chanting an angry "Ah" sound over and over.

"Are you ok?" I asked.

"Ahhhhhh. Ahhhhh, just get out. Get your things and leave! God, this is so fucked!" Colin watched us now rather than the TV, his eyes totally blank, as I walked past and grabbed my bag. "Nice knowing you," I said to the silent Mya, as I walked out of her apartment and into the dark hall. It wasn't the best day I'd ever had and certainly not what I'd expected. Descending into a sun that was strong and in my eyes, I looked left, then right and then left and right once again. I looked for a pay phone, to call my sister. She needed to know that I was in town and that she could expect a visitor.

Andy Henion

Brogan's Summer Break

Brogan hunts for rodent feces in his cereal. Joey Pena at school told him the government allows so many parts per something, so he dumps out half the box and works the tweezers, hunched over the pile like a tiny scientist, eyes plump behind pop bottle lenses. Aardvark the dog sits statue-still at his side, waiting for a piece to fall, feces or no.

His brother Ryan enters through the sliding door, followed by Tahara. Ryan grins and says, "Wheezer's looking for rat shit again," and Tahara, whom Brogan cannot look at without feeling funny inside, says, "I'll help." She leans over the table and even though Brogan enjoys her bronze skin and coconut scent he pays special attention to the pieces she touches because he will not eat Lucky Charms tainted with another's finger oil and germs, even Tahara's.

Ryan says, "Where's Mom?" Brogan examines two more pieces before looking up, adjusting his horn-rims and saying, "First of all, cease the Wheezer. Second of all, Mom's at AA." He returns to his task and Ryan touches Tahara's arm and says, C'mon. He leads her down the hallway and into his bedroom, throwing a wink over his shoulder.

Brogan continues the hunt for several minutes but fails to identify the offending matter. He feeds the contaminated cereal to Aardvark, scoops the rest into the box and starts down the hall. Aardvark lopes ahead, attracted by the giggling, and noses open the door. Ryan has left it cracked.

While the dog garners the couple's attention, Brogan drops to his belly and army-crawls to the bed. There he turns over and slithers underneath until his nose is an inch from the mattress springs. Above him Tahara complains about the dog sitting there watching, to which Ryan laughs and says, "He's here to learn from the master. Get it? The master."

The thing about Brogan's older brother, he's a smooth one. A ladies man. There's always guys in the basement listening to his senior year exploits. Just the other day he told them he was fucking Tahara and one of them said, "No way, your cousin?" and Ryan winked and said, "*Third* cousin. And she's adopted." At that point he motioned at Brogan, sitting dangle-legged on the washing machine, and said, "If you tools can keep your mouths shut I'll let the Wheezer watch next time and fill you in."

Soon the mattress is springing toward Brogan and his brother is grunting as if angry. Brogan didn't know fucking was this violent. A deformed piece of spring begins ticking against the right lens of his spectacles, lightly at first but then hard enough to scar the glass, and Brogan knows he should turn his head but instead slips into a trance with the rhythmic *tick-tick-tick* and eventually falls asleep and dreams of his father, whom he never knew, chasing Tahara through the underground tunnels of a place called Cambodia.

*

Brogan aims his BB gun at Seth Berber. But the scratched lens forces him to pause and adjust his glasses, and Seth gets off the first shot. The BB strikes Brogan in the neck, just south of the adam's apple, and he drops his weapon and falls to the street. There is pain, accelerated breathing, and Brogan tries to pull out his inhaler but the damn thing slips and gets lost underneath him as he writhes on the asphalt.

Seth Barber runs to his house yelling something about Brogan dying. He returns with his dad who has him by the collar and an angry look on his face. His father says, "Goddamn kids," and reaches down and flips Brogan over. He retrieves his inhaler, slams it in his mouth and pumps, but Brogan is not prepared and motions frantically for Seth Barber's dad to do it again, and again. Finally he feels the medicine open his passage and at this point Seth Barber's dad orders Seth into the house and then grabs Brogan by the upper arm and spanks him hard on the ass right there in the middle of

Oakleaf Lane. "Since you don't have a dad," he says, whaling away, "I'll do it for you. Little fuckin' idiot."

*

Brogan growls at the man in the eyeglass store. He growls lightly so his mother cannot hear but he growls nonetheless, curling his lip and baring his teeth. Although Brogan has never met this man, he knows him, has known a dozen like him—men who come after his mom like sharks for the wounded. Brogan knows his mother is as vulnerable as she is beautiful, four months sober and each day a battle.

"Little man's a tiger," says the man. He's absurdly tall with a thin neck and sharp bones. He draws near, as Brogan knew he would. They always start with the kid.

Brogan says, "Little man's got turrets, epilepsy, various other conditions." To prove his point he produces a line of drool and a series of tics.

The man makes a surprised face, looks around. Brogan's mother is across the room examining frames while they wait for Brogan's new lens. "And a comedian to boot," says the man. He reaches out to chuck Brogan's chin; Brogan draws away and says, "Sir, don't touch me."

Brogan's mother is making her way over with a pair of glasses. He knows he has to speak fast, so he says, "Listen, Ace, I know what you're after, but know this: She's needy, controlling and close to bankruptcy. No gravy train here."

The man barks. His mother's eyes turn to slits. When she reaches them she wipes the saliva from Brogan's chin with a thumb and forefinger—the only person allowed to touch him—and says, "What did you say to the man?"

Brogan opens his mouth to respond but the man does it for him. "Little man's just making convo." As if taking his side: another standard technique.

Brogan's mother says "Uh-huh," as if she doesn't believe the man, and holds up the frames, thick and black. "Nice horn-rims," says Brogan. His mother nods and looks over at the man. He smiles crookedly, and in that smile Brogan sees the future: the man's underwear in the laundry piles, his shaky, hung-over laughter at the breakfast table, his mother's vodka bottle back in the fridge door, poorly hidden behind the ketchup and mayonnaise.

*

Brogan discovers masturbation on a Friday afternoon. It's not the penis-in-palm variety but a two-fingered rub through his sweatpants. This being his first time he does not know what's coming, and when it comes he's at first terrified, and then repulsed. Lifting the waistband of his sweatpants, he sees the sticky white gel and is up and scrambling for the shower, gagging at the smell. After ten minutes under a near-boiling spray he gets himself under control and proceeds to slip on his mother's rubber gloves and deposit the mucky sweatpants deep in the kitchen trash.

No one comes home this evening—his mother is camping with the tall man; Ryan is out doing his fucking—and Brogan eventually comes to grips with what he's done. He accepts it as a function of his flawed mortality but resolves to keep it as hygienic as possible. So the next time, two hours later, he completes the act in the shower with strawberry shampoo to mask the odor. Brogan closes his eyes and thinks of Tahara's dark skin in a white bikini, and over the remaining days and weeks of summer he will take so many showers his skin will pucker like a pale grape.

*

Brogan scorches a cockroach with the man's torch. The man is a welding instructor at the community college, whatever that means, and last week did a five-minute repair job on the water heater, Brogan studying the procedure closely from the staircase. So when his mother and the man disappear for yet another weekend, he commandeers the portable welding apparatus from the basement—where the man is storing boxes upon boxes of his junk—and lugs it into the back yard. There he stands a chunk of firewood upright, hunts down a series of insects and fries them crisp. Although he has read any number of books in which the serial killer starts out slaughtering insects and small domestic animals, Brogan is confident he does not fit this mold. He's interested in a career in science or medicine, after all, and thus pays special attention to the color and amount of blood that spills from his subjects.

In the empty lot next door rages a baseball game. Joey Pena is playing. So is Seth Barber. The last time Brogan was allowed to play he struck out three times and when he finally did make contact—a fluke liner to right field—he misjudged second base, tripped and was tagged out, costing Kyle Masterson's team the game. Kyle Masterson subsequently berated Brogan in front of the crew and then knocked him face-first into the hard-packed field, bloodying his nose. Kyle Masterson is the reason Brogan refuses to ride the school bus or venture into the neighborhood without his big brother. Kyle Masterson is a motherfucker.

The ball suddenly lands near Brogan's experiment. He looks up to see Kyle Masterson standing about twenty feet away. He says, "Throw it back, Bro*tard*." Brogan, in a fit of something foreign to him, picks up the ball, flings it the other way and says, "Go fetch, bitch." He immediately recognizes the silence—the dead stillness—of the previously boisterous baseball players. Kyle Masterson is not still, however; he's coming for Brogan with a maniacal grin. "Big brother's not around now, *bitch*." Brogan frantically picks up the welding torch, adjusts the knob so the flame burns full and points it at Kyle Masterson.

Who does not slow down. He says, "What are you gonna do, *cook me*?" and puts his first baseman's glove over the flame, effectively neutralizing Brogan's advantage. Brogan takes a step back, but it's too late: Kyle Masterson punches him in the chest. Brogan gasps and drops to a knee, digging out his inhaler. Kyle Masterson kicks it out of his hand. Brogan half-stands and begins hunting for his life support, turning circles like a hunched over, wheezing old man. He hears Kyle Masterson's laughter. He hears other voices beyond. He falls to his side, throat closing like a vice, black spots taking over his vision, and never sees who it is that saves him.

*

Brogan learns of his mother's engagement over breakfast. "The wedding's in six weeks," she says, waggling her fingers to show off the ring. "We're finally gonna be a family, boys." Ryan, in that ultra cool way of his, says, "Great, Ma, I'm happy for you." It's easy for him to say; he's off to college on a wrestling scholarship. Brogan feels anything but happy. He wants to say, "We *are* a family," but instead lets it sit inside him like a cold stone.

Later, when everyone has gone, Brogan sneaks into his mother's room, Aardvark close on his heels. He sits on the bed, removes his new glasses and proceeds to paint his face: blush, mascara, lipstick. Then he pulls on one of his mother's best dresses, a pastel yellow number that gathers around his feet. "Dearly beloved," he says to the dog, "do you take this welding instructor even though he's an asshole?" He reapplies his glasses, lifts the dress to his knees and marches through the house chanting military cadence. *"I want to be an airborne ranger,"* he says, which is actually true if a career in medicine doesn't work out. By that point in life Brogan plans to be asthma-free and wearing contacts, just like Ryan. Maybe he'll even attend fighter pilot school.

Next stop is Ryan's room where, in the sock drawer, he finds pictures of Tahara naked. In one of them she has her backside hiked up revealing a hairy mound with a mysterious fold. She has a finger in the fold. Brogan stares at the picture so intently he turns lightheaded and stumbles into his room for a shot off the inhaler. Then it's out of the dress and into the shower for thirty seconds of frantic activity, his mother's makeup rolling down his sunken chest as his jism swirls down the drain.

*

Brogan watches a movie with his big brother Ryan. It's by far the best night of the summer, a tub of popcorn in his lap and an ass-kicking superhero on the big screen. Ryan is sprawled back in his seat as two girls toss popcorn at him. When a kernel falls on his chest or shoulders he picks it off and eats it, never losing that blasé smile and never once looking at the girls. This, Brogan knows, is what drives them crazy.

On the walk home Ryan says, "So how's it been going?"

Brogan is practicing his thunder punches, imagining that he's saving his father from evil-eyed soldiers in the Cambodian prison camp. Snapping a fist into the air, he says, in his deep superhero's voice, "Solid."

The girls are a block behind them, singing Ryan's name into pop tunes. Brogan wishes his brother would tell them to get lost.

"Solid, huh? So what's this about you wearing mom's dresses and putting on her makeup?"

Brogan stops in mid-punch. Stands straight. Adjusts his glasses. Scratches the back of his neck.

"No big deal," says Ryan. He pulls out a can of snuff, drops a pinch into his cheek. The girls have stopped in front of a house and are standing arm-in-arm, making pouty faces. Ryan finally looks back at them, shakes his head and says, "Sophomores." A passing car honks and two high-schoolers lean out and shout Ryan's name. Brogan can't help but think his brother is the most popular kid in town.

"So what do you think about the new guy?" Ryan says.

"Dillweed," says Brogan. His brother's term.

"You think? Do you know he played minor league baseball?"

Brogan didn't know this, or perhaps didn't care to remember. To him, the tall man's words are so much background noise. He's a *welder*, for crying out loud.

"He can teach you to play ball," Ryan says. The unspoken truth is that he never liked baseball, never found much time to play catch with his younger brother. The few times they did Brogan would throw it three feet over his head, unable to gauge the proper height.

The girls are heading into the house, teasing Ryan about his last chance. He says, "You make it home?" It's only three blocks, there's plenty of light, but still Brogan purses his lips and hunches his shoulders.

"C'mon, Wheezer," says Ryan, backpedaling. "You wouldn't deny your brother his freak-on?"

Brogan is not familiar with a freak-on. He does know about sexually transmitted diseases, however, and says, "You're gonna mess around and get those AIDS, fella."

Ryan laughs the laugh of the invincible and glides down the sidewalk.

*

Brogan slips under the table with a plastic cup of beer. He does so as the guests are clinking their glasses to get his mother and the tall man to make out for the hundredth time. It's dark under the table, tissue paper providing cover, and he risks a quick drink, wincing from the bitterness. The crowd cheers, none louder than fat Aunt Jenny to his immediate left. She's from Pennsylvania; to his right is Cousin Somebody-or-other from Ohio. Before long they're talking in the space Brogan just occupied about how happy his mother is. How oddly similar the groom looks to Brogan's father, God bless his soul. Brogan takes a large slug of beer and gags, vomiting a bit back into his mouth.

The discussion turns to Tahara. She's a dead ringer for her mother, God bless her soul. A stunning young woman. At this point they go quiet and Brogan realizes

Tahara must have been approaching them all along, and is here now. "Have you guys seen Brogan?" she asks. This is followed by small talk, questions about how this part of the family or that part of the family has been doing. Then, silence. What Brogan doesn't know is that the relatives are motioning under the table.

The paper comes up slowly to reveal high heels; Tahara's bent, bare legs extending out of a white dress; her oval face. Brogan goes woozy in her presence, ears flush, thoughts wiped clean.

"You want to dance when you're done with that?"

Brogan forgot he was holding the plastic cup. He sets it on the floor next to him, making sure not to touch the grimy carpet, and says, "I don't know how."

"*Slow* dance," says Tahara, extending a hand. "C'mon, handsome."

He walks with her to the dance floor, feeling the eyes upon them, and instinctively fingers the inhaler in his pocket. The song starts—something about sailing on down the line—and Tahara guides his hands to her waist and gently takes his shoulders. They dance like that, in slow circles, and after a few moments she says, "So how'd your summer go?" and Brogan, feeling more confident now, says, "Solid." To which she smiles and says, "I like your new glasses. When did you get those?" Brogan thinks back to the day under Ryan's bed, to his brother doing his fucking on Tahara, and now, well, where the hell is he? Over there dancing with some other girl as if Tahara didn't matter—just another one of his conquests.

He says, simply, "Few weeks ago."

Tahara moves close and rests her head on his shoulder. Their bodies press. She's hard and soft at the same time, smells of something wonderful—flowers, maybe, or vanilla. Feeling the stab of her nipples, her breath on his neck, Brogan hardens. He starts to shift his hips away, but she pulls him back. "It's okay," she whispers. "That's what happens."

*

Brogan fires the baseball at the tall man's nuts. He has no legitimate reason to be angry—Brogan has misread him, after all; the man is no drunk, no freeloader—yet still he fires. As usual, the ball sails high, destined for the vacant lot until his new stepfather sticks up his glove and snatches it out of the air.

"Nice arm," he says. "Just get it down."

School starts tomorrow. High school. Kyle Masterson has promised to make this a year Brogan will never forget, the fucker. Brogan clenches his teeth and hurls the ball even harder, satisfied with the *pop* it makes in the tall man's glove.

"Better," he says.

Tahara is a senior this year; Brogan will walk the halls with her. He wonders if she'll acknowledge him. He wonders if he she'll wear that white dress to school. He wonders she would ever do some secret fucking with him, someone who would treat her right.

"Strike," says the tall man. "Throw that fuckin' smoke, kid."

Ms. Jean Kang

Sewer Rat: Queen of the Damned

A few days ago I met Italo Pompa of Pescara, Italia, at Dam Square in Amsterdam. According to this Tunisian I met on a bus, Italo Pompa is a fake name. It is somehow vulgar. We hung out for a day and when he left for Italy I gave him 20 euros for the train. We parted at Central Station. The night before we slept outdoors at the docks where the houseboats float on the water. Morning came and I was supposed to leave for Italy for the Venice Biennale, but I never made it there. Instead I walked around the city some more and I ran into Henson, this kid from Senegal who has an intelligent face and deals drugs because he's an illegal immigrant (though he'd rather be a musician). He gave me some ecstasy and wanted me to go to his home and hang out but I wanted to stay free and keep moving.

I decided to take a bus to Venice since it would be cheaper. The bus station was in Utrecht, so I hopped on the night train and slept in the station.

That morning at Amstel Station, I met a man named Rudy from Surinam.

I must have looked pathetic to him. He told me he watched me wake up and wander over to the kiosk where he was standing in line for coffee. He bought me a coffee and a pastry, and asked me if I'd join him for a smoke. I was out of cigarettes, so I followed him through the station, which was part of a large indoor mall.

He handed me a cigarette, then said: I will buy two bags of coke: One for me, one for you. I like you. You are my queen.

I'm not making this up.

Outside the air smelled like piss and there were all these junkies scurrying about in the back parking lot. We were in the loading dock and somehow the scene looked post apocalyptic in a biblical way, with all these dirty lepers sitting on the stairs getting high and these fat crack dealers holding up baggies for sale. The scene seemed too staged for my taste. It was a gritty marketplace for people with open sores.

I wanted to head back to the station, but Rudy asked me to stay with him for just one smoke. I agreed because I had time to kill, and, I suppose, because I didn't mind having a hit of crack just before a 31-hour bus ride. He took me up a hill behind these trees overlooking the town and I was scared but only mildly so. He seemed harmless and was too enamored with me to really hurt me.

I love you, he said. You are mine.

I told him I was married and he asked me if he was a good man. Oh yes he is I said.

And your man, does he smoke?

Only the good stuff.

Good, said Rudy, then we will smoke together and you and your husband both will come live with me and I will show you my family, my mother and sister, and if you want I will whore you out for lots of money and buy you the best heroin that money can buy, and if your husband shoots, I will let him shoot and I will buy you a clean needle and cotton and fuck you both. Your husband, I hope, takes it up the ass.

I think he does, I said.

Good, he smiled. And now, I will fix you a big hit but you must take it from my mouth.

This I refused and made up a story about how I believe in monogamy.

But I love you, he said.

I love you too, and if I were with you I wouldn't be with anyone else.

But as for me, he said, when I smoke I need to play with somebody so you must take it from my mouth.

I forgot to tell you how, just before all this, the conversation turned, and he was telling me about being in prison for seven years for killing a man. I was afraid he'd rape or kill me so I went along with him. But since he kept insisting he was in love with me, I was sure I had the upper hand.

I need this to be happy, he said.

I remember thinking how strange it was to look below and see people riding by on their bicycles. It was a regular workday. These were normal people leading regular lives. They were immaculate visions of health and normalcy, something that I craved.

But I was high and feeling like Oprah. I was no longer afraid, though I did want another hit off his pipe. All the same, he had my sympathy: He was so addicted.

I ended up counseling him: You don't need anything to be happy, at least not crack. You're better off without the drug, I said. It's okay if you've killed a man. That's all in your past. Just don't do it again. But this business with the crack cocaine must stop.

He gave me his mother's phone number and told me to call him as soon as I can. He was hugging me, crying. For you I will do anything. You are my queen. I was embarrassed for him, this 50-year-old man. And so I held his hand and cradled his head as I took the smoke from his lips. He wanted to buy two more bags, but I told him I had a bus to catch. He insisted he walk me to the station and sit with me while I wait. I told him this was unnecessary. He bought me a bottle of water. I remember turning around as I entered the bus station: He was standing at the gate of the parking lot, bawling.

Adam P. Knave

Two Drunk Minimum

I went to this bar the other night. Met a girl. You know, we hit it off decently, nothing too magical but it was a nice enough time. She looked really fucking familiar but I couldn't quite place where I had seen her before, you know?

So we're sitting there, at this little dive bar, *Lou's*, for about three hours. We're sitting and talking and drinking for a while. She leans more towards scotch, hard liquor and small shots, while I stray back towards the beer families more often than not. Sometimes we would meet up around vodka, but we drank where the conversation took us.

Anyway, after a while, we were both good and pickled and I looked at her and yelped. Like a little fucking yappy dog with those big stupid fucking ears, I yelped. I yelped and I sat back a bit, swaying impressively on my stool.

"Hey, I know you," I told her, surprise still having its way with my lobes.

She laughed a flat laugh, the laugh of a drunk and nodded at me.

"O'course you do. We've been talking for hours!" She changed the nod to a headshake midstream and a brief moment of confusion and possible expulsion creased her face, the change in direction upsetting her carefully balanced system.

"No, no, before that, before all that. You..." I thought about it and sat up straighter, trying to look like I knew what I was doing, like I was *sober*, "You're that bearded, elephant trunked siamese twin from the circus, right?" My words hit her like blows. Large punches delivered by marshmallow peeps. All candy yellow and pink, sugar coating flying off like angel dust as they collided with her face.

"Joe, man, come on. Do I look like a bearded elephant trunked siamese twin to you?" Her voice purred at me, her spine arched and she lifted her scotch to me, downing it with vigor. "Can't we just have a good time?" I shook my head and stood up to leave.

"The cops are after you, Doll. I suggest you get a move on. Just like I am." I sighed and paid the tab, a sucker once again.

"The next guy might not be fooled just 'cause you shave." I slunk out of the bar and back towards home, annoyed at myself. The City's lights sparkled above me and onto me as I wound my way back to my small apartment.

Stephen Moran

Time Out, Carmencita

Me probation officer talked me into it, putting an advert in Time Out. I was lonely, and I thought what harm is there in it, and I thought I might as well be above board about things, for once in me life, you get nowhere by sitting in your homeless B&B room watching I'm a Gobshite, Let me Out of Here, and eating batch loaf by the handful.

Mature Irish lady, well-set, late of HMP Holloway, seeks male companion 40-60, G.S.O.H, possibly another ex-offender, for outings and possible romance.

I didn't get very many replies, and they were mostly too far away, so I was wondering should I put what I was in for, embezzling from the Little Sisters of the Poor, but I thought that'd only be worse.

Then one local one came through to the box number, so I thought jaze here we go girls, and all the way there

I couldn't get that song, 'If you like Pina Colada' out of me head, y'know the one where yer man and yer woman meet, though they're all Yanks and rich as Lords' bastards, heaven forgive me, I've an awful mouth on me. 'If you're not into yoga' – for jazesake, it'd take a JCB to get me into some of them positions.

And I'm wondering what'll he be like – I mean he already told me in his reply he's an ex-offender like meself, so he can have nothing to complain about on that score. I knew the minute I laid eyes on him he was a weirdo, and don't they always wear grey raincoats and keep their hands down in their pockets – and to tell you the truth, I like to see what a man's hands are up to at all times. And I'm not that gone on the little moustaches, you know the ones does be thinking they look like Clark Gable with the centipede on their lip.

And then he opens his mouth and d'y'know what? I nearly wet meself. How I kept a straight face I'll never know. What it was, his voice was that high, I swear if it was any higher only dogs could hear it.

'Pleased to meet you,' says he.

Jesus, Mary and Joseph I must've gone puce in the face, and you know what I'm like, I mean Nina Simone isn't in it, so between the two of us it was like *Mammy sang bass and Daddy sang tenor.* Holy feckin name a jazes.

'Good evening,' says I and quick-thinking how to talk about something serious, 'What were you in for?'

'Oh now, that'd be telling,' says he.

'If you're a pervert, tell me now and there's another train in two minutes,' (we were on a platform) 'and I'll be on it.'

'What?' says he. 'Can you define that?'

'Define me arse,' says I.

'Well I might be a pervert and been in for murder or vice-versa, and which would be worse?'

'Cheerio!' says I, and the train pulling in.

'Ah wait,' says he. 'Forgery.'

'Oh why didn't you say – that's all right then. And you're not a pervert?'

'I didn't say that,' says he. 'Are you?'

'Well, you imper'ent get!' says I. 'I'll have you know I'm a country girl.'

'Sure what difference does that make,' says he. 'Is there no perverts in the country?'

'Me brother has a shotgun.'

That shut him up till he said, 'You missed your train.'

'Oh you're very witty. Are we going for this drink or what?'

So we're sitting in the Spotted Dog, the Gaelic Lounge, before it became the Sindrome this was, and he's got the one half lager top, and I'm on me third pint - and he's not bad company now, I'll say that for him, he'd make you laugh – but you'd still want to pretend you weren't with him. And he still hasn't asked me what I was in for, says he doesn't care.

'Here,' says I, 'Do you not like the booze here or what?'

'It's me stomach,' says he. 'I've an ulcer the size of a victoria plum.'

'Would you stop,' says I, 'you're putting me off me stout.'

Now he was like a stick insect, I'm not coddin you, I'd be afraid if I sat on him I'd break him, that's the gospel. Anyhow, doesn't he start a coughing fit, and holy lantern a-jazes it'd give you the screaming habdabs, the hawking and gurgling and drawn-out spitting into a feckin handkerchief. Well J-Cloth should investigate that feckin rag because it must've absorbed about a pint of slobber and snot, God forgive me.

'Ah for Christ's sake – do you want me to call an ambulance or what?'

Well he just waved - you know the way – because he was still coughing.

'Is your friend alright?' says the barmaid, Australian girl.

'He's not *my* friend,' I said - I know it's a sin, and him still waving not to get the ambulance, and the sort of horrified look that passed over his face when I said that. What the feck have I got meself into here, I'm thinking, when doesn't he keel over and clatters over and out of the chair.

'What are you looking at?' I says to the barmaid. 'I'm not feckin giving him the kiss of life.'

Jerry Springer was on the telly, and I was wondering if he did a London special would he consider featuring 'Me boyfriend choked to death on our first date.' I was lying on me single bed in the B&B, with the Time Out beside me. I thought about changing the words in the advert, but no I'd just make sure I knew what the next person had been inside for.

As an embezzler meself (I know it's a sin, and from the Little Sisters of the Poor too) I don't mean to be snobby, but I just feel more at home with fellas in a financial line of work, not necessarily "something in the city," could be something in the bank or something in the post office. It'd do no harm if they'd done a million pound con job and stashed the money away somewhere. Anything not involving sex, drugs or violence in other words, the better class of criminal, ones you'd nearly boast about at a party.

Did you hear about our uncle Noel? The one with the villa in Spain. Done for fraud. Sold 100 one month timeshares in it for £5,000 a go. Oh he's not short of a few bob. As cute as a bag of ferrets. Sure he'll be out in about eighteen months, it's only like a rest cure for him, and a chance to write his book "The Timeshare King."

Anyway the next fella, another munchkin – jaze, I'm saying to meself, what do they think I am, or are all little dwarves chubby-chasers or what? A nice respectable looking chap, all the same, well dressed. Set up his own charity, only the pigs, I mean Scotland Yard, didn't see it that way.

Same as last time, we talked about what we did, and him looking down his nose, if that's possible from below, at me fiddling books at the convent. Too petty for him, you see. The more I looked at him, the more I was thinking I know beggars can't be choosers, but still, this geezer must've been in his sixties at least, and me being only fifty.

So we went to see Evita the musical, no expense spared, fair play to him, and there's this coffin on the stage at the beginning, so it sets me thinking and I asked him in his ear, 'Is your health okay?'

'Got a dicky ticker,' he sort of mouths, half whispers, and taps his chest.

At the same time as I'm thinking this ould shite is too old for me, another part of me is thinking 'Lauren Bacall me, I want to be rainbow high.' God forgive me. I wondered if he had insurance. 'Next stop is going to be Europe.' Tra la la.

Corbin, his name was, would you believe, and full of himself he was. Afterwards in this fancy Chinese restaurant with the waitresses in red silk dresses and all, and here's he lecturing me on history and news, and it was all I could do not to yawn. He reminded me of one of them Open University lecturers does be on the telly late at night, better than Mogadon for knocking you out.

Next minute what is it only his foot half way up me leg. Jaze, at first I thought what a clumsy clodhopper, and shifted meself, then next minute here he is again up to me feckin thigh. Ah here, I says to meself, this is a randy old goat. And the funniest thing is, he's still eating, concentrating on his food, as if his foot had a life of its own. I'm thinking for feck sake, he'll dirty me tights with his shoes, and I glance under the table and hasn't he got his shoe off, and this'll give you a laugh – no socks on. Crazy horses!

There he is fiddling with his noodles with the chopsticks and here's his foot tiddling me inner thighs. It was so strange I looked around just to make sure it wasn't somebody else coming at me from behind, like. Well I stopped eating for a while, but I thought what the hell, and I started back to shovelling the special fried rice into me face, and I said two can play at that game and dropped a high heel and put me foot straight over into his crotch. I don't know what possessed me.

He half-choked on something and muttered, 'England nil, Republic of Ireland one' (this is the God's honest truth) and there's me palpating his stalk through the worsted suit, and then he starts what sounds like praying, y'know, his lips moving and words like, 'Holy Mother pray for me, St Francis of Assisi forgive me, saints and angels preserve me. Immaculate Mother interceeeeede for me!'

I'm thinkin is this a feckin priest or what - for jazesake, I just can't win. By this time his foot was dinging me panties now like, and here's a funny thing, the food tasted fantastic, it was like the most delicious juices and morsels lindy-hopping and doing the watusi on me taste buds. The two of us had the same thought at the same time, when the waiter came near us. 'Can we get a doggy bag?'

Corbin should've been the making of me, but the way it was I was lucky to get out of that without a post-release licence violation. It's not a bit funny. Nearly put the heart crossways in me he did, when I realised he wasn't just in dreamland, on his pink flannelette sheets in a creaky old bed that went out with the ark, it was a dead weight I was bouncing, literally.

If I'd played me cards right I'd be the merry widow by now, several times over, but muggins here of course, never thinking about meself always other people, probation officers, screws, policemen, auditors - and not as if one of them ever gave a damn about me.

This was getting a bit of a bore, dead old codgers everywhere under me feet, so I changed the ad. *Fit, mature (or would consider immature) companion. Would suit weightlifter*, I put. But I was cagey enough. What I'd do I'd spy on them before meeting and if they looked any way feeble I'd stand them up, I thought.

I gave up meeting on the platform because it was too hard to hide there and observe. Outside the station was better because I could sit in the café opposite and see what they looked like first. Or so I thought. Here's me o.d'ing on cappucino and the only people I see are scrawny kids who are not there five minutes till another gang of kids appears and off they go. Where's the logic in standing somebody up on a blind date? And it was all confirmed now, y'know, that he'd be carrying a newspaper.

And then I notice this horsefaced geezer with unsuccessful whiskers, at a table the other side of the door and reading a paper, moryah, but gawking all the time at everyone coming and going outside the station opposite. A sleeveen. I'm not the least bit hard to please, but if there's one thing I can't stand, it's a sly go-by-the-wall type of get. Anyway he looked like Johnny Fortycoats or a wino or one of those smelly oulfellas does have allotments and smokes pipes. I'm not that desperate. I thought here, I'm getting out before he starts looking at me.

I paid the Greek gentleman for the use of his coffee and wandered out a there with me umbrella – like a proper Charlie, and the sun splitting the stones, but that was me sign, like his was the newspaper, and I'm so full of meself, delighted the plan saved me from an evening with Catweazel, that I says I'll celebrate and treat meself to a one-and-one, forgetting that I'm passing through the danger zone in front of the station to get to the chip shop.

Holy mother, next thing here's yer man shouting at me from across the road and me pretending not to hear him, thinking I'll go to the next chippy along the high road – which I did, and it was gorgeous, I must admit, but by rights I should be strung up for a callous bitch. I must have a heart of stone, because I felt nothing about the accident. I mean it wasn't my fault the dopey shite ran out under the number 256. He was too hairy anyway. Brrrrrr! Gives me the willies even thinking about it. Imagine waking up next to that? He's better off out of it, God forgive me.

I was lucky enough to get a job doing housekeeper for Father Santos in St. Buthold's, after the lady who used to do it had to go into hospital with her kidneys. Minnie her name was, terrible nice, under Doctor Banister.

I thought I'd never do anything again, I'd learned me lesson. Fr Santos'd leave the odd fiver lying around and forget about it, but I wouldn't lay a finger on it. I'd watch it for weeks like, but you see it could be a trap. Anyway priests would forget their heads if they weren't screwed on. Not like the nuns, bejaze, that lot'd be hard cessed to part with a dollar to save their lives.

I hadn't much to do because Fr Santos liked to do his own cooking and household things, very neat and tidy he was, from Manila no less. There nothing he liked better than getting his marigolds on and dusting, and he always had some foul-smelling, foreign muck on cooking. And here's me twiddling me thumbs with nothing to do but answer the phone and show people into his office. He'd be that miserable when I'd interrupt him listening to Lea Salonga on his headphones (Miss Saigon, she was) that half the time I'd volunteer to deal with the people meself and leave him waltzing around with his feather duster like a gobdaw.

It got to the stage where he didn't want to talk to anyone, I'd have to deal with them all meself, and he didn't want me to touch anything in the house or the kitchen. He used to call me his verger. If anyone complained he'd say, "That's a matter for Mrs Haverty, the verger." (The 'Mrs' is only an honorary title, by the way, people call me that because of my age and I can't be arsed explaining all the time.)

Of course it was a good arrangement because I was more in tune with the problems of the locals, they were mostly Irish like meself – well if they weren't I gave them short shrift, though you had to show willing and hem and haw but generally I'd more or less give them the bum's rush. I mean do they not have their own churches? I shouldn't say that, I know.

What I was really on the lookout for was a nice widower, on his last legs, from one of the big million pound houses in Brondesbury. Well you couldn't blame me. I didn't want to be a housekeeper forever, the only career path in it was to the NHS hospital and from there into a pauper's grave, me being an orphan with no rich relatives to leave me anything, by the way, in case you think I'm just putting on the poor mouth.

Father Santos let me move into a room in the presbytery on condition that I never let any of my things out of the room. I had to hang me washing in there and all, for jazesake, he got queasy about the thought of women's underwear. It was just as well because the duties of looking after the parish were taking all me time. The only thing Fr Santos did was to say Mass, that was the only part he liked, dressing up, dancing around the altar and being the centre of attention.

It shook me up something awful, it did, when Fr Santos got electrocuted. If I'd told him once, I'd told him a hundred times not to use the steel knife to poke the bread out of the toaster when it got stuck, and of course him always being in his bare feet didn't help.

What the hell was I going to do? The new priest wasn't a bit like Fr Santos. I could tell he wanted rid of me, though the mealy-mouthed religion made him bottle it up. He was one of those shiny-faced, smirking fellas does have a way of looking at something behind or beside you or closing their eyes half the time when they're talking. Father Tierney his name was.

I'd been thinking I was at least secure as a housekeeper in St Buthold's, and I was able to live in a bit of style for a while, by lightening a few of the envelopes with the dues. But Lord Muck was crowding me out, never giving me a chance to continue my pastoral work, nor nothing. If anybody said they wanted to speak with the verger (me), he'd turn up his nose and say something like, 'Oh Mrs Haverty is far too busy with the hoovering and whatever else she does here. She is one of the divine mysteries - we just have to take her on faith.'

Feck you, I thought – pardon my French – I'll not stay where I'm not wanted. I'd had a sickener with the Time Out ads, so it occurred to me to try something different. My friend Stella McCusker came up with this idea of going to a pub in Tottenham Court Road where singles went, a singles bar, for the over 21's.

Come Saturday night and here's me in scarlet lipstick and matching dress, with heavy duty high heels and tights with a ladder in them out of sight, stopped with a dab of nail varnish. The neck on the ould M&S dress was a bit low – not that I was getting desperate now – but what the hell – if you've got it flaunt it. I looked like ould Two Ton Titty O'Shea.

It was Stella who talked me into this and here's the two of us walking into this place, the Knacker's Arms it was called (nearly all pubs in London have names like that, Christ knows why) and half-expecting it to be full of youngsters and us dressed up like mutton.

'For fecksake,' she says, 'it's more like a geriatric visiting ward than a singles bar.'

Stella is only a little doll, but she has a mouth on her like a trooper, she'd crack you up, honestly.

'Never mind,' says I, shushing her. 'There's many a good tune played on an old fiddle.'

'Fiddle is right,' says she. 'I'd say there's plenty of fiddlers here.'

Well jazes, I'm not codding you, she'd have you in knots. But right enough, the last time I saw that much white hair was when Fr Santos (God rest him) took the Derby and Joan club on their annual outing to Margate, and half of them had heart attacks on the Mary Rose. For jazesake, compared to some of them we were like Blue Peter presenters. Stop!

I thought better of ordering a pint, and had a cocktail instead, a Suicide Car Bomb I think it was called and it looked and tasted like cloudy piss, I'd say, not that I'd know. Gahd! Stella had a Gin and It. She said she'd always wanted to find out what the "it" was. Well she was none the wiser after because the barman was Estonian or something and their conversation'd give you the heebie jeebies.

Says Stella, 'A Gin and It, please.'

'Okay,' and he gave her the drink.

'And can I just ask,' she sort of whispers.

'Yes?'

'What is the "it"?'

'What is the it?'

'I mean the it in gin and it.'

'Yes. I give you gin and it.'

'I know.'

'You have problem?'

'No, it's just I've always wondered, what is the it, the it in gin and it, what does the it in it mean. The it?'

'Yes. Gin and it.'

We're on barstools now, and this moustachey-faced Howard Keel lookylikey next door to Stella says something like, '*Sweek vermousk.*'

'Oh for fecksake! Give it up Stella, nobody here speaks English. *Spasiva*,' says I, thinking most of these refugees does know Russian.

'Don't mention it,' says he. 'Peter Hurley. And you young ladies are- ?'

'Are what?' says I, me dander rising.

'Stella and Carmen,' says Stella and gives me a kick in the shin, that still comes back and twinges me to this day.

'*Enchantée*,' says he and takes Stella's arm and kisses it. I could see Stella looking him up and down, with his silver-buttoned blazer and his Hush Puppies. I'm thinking, great, Stella has pulled and here's yours truly the gooseberry, when he reaches across her and lifts up my hand and tickles me wrist with his ronnie. I snorted and went red. I felt such a pig, y'know, I can't help it, but it didn't bother him.

'D'y'know what,' says he, 'I don't know which of you is the most beautiful.'

'You must be blind as well as thick,' I said under me breath.

'I think,' says he, 'between the two of you, you could teach me a lot. I don't mean to be forward but I have a lovely place in Hampstead – jacuzzi, sauna, the works. Can I tempt you ladies to join me there for a nightcap.'

There's Stella with her jaw dropped, and me getting the giggles. The only thing I knew about nightcaps was *upstairs, downstairs and in his lady's chamber...*

'Wee Willy Winky!' I spluttered and spat half the mouthful of drink I'd just taken and the other half up me nose. Talk about bringing tears to your eyes, the feckin drink came out of me eyes I think.

'I'll drive you there in my Bentley and drop you home after.'

Say no more. Stella swallowed her drink in one gulp, and had her coat on and me still laughing.

You know I miss Stella, God knows I do, but this is it, I should've gone with them. It's eating me up. I know you'll say if "ifs and ands" were pots and pans, something something something. This is it. Never drink and drive.

Meanwhile Fr Tierney was getting a bit, what would you say, frisky. I'm no prude now, but there's really only space for me to go through a doorway as long as there's nobody else there, you know what I mean. He had a bad habit of standing in the way and making me squeeze past. With them being celibate you see, it preys on their minds, and they miss not so much the how's-your-father, just the contact, y'know. They touch nobody and nobody touches them. Even when they give you the host onto your tongue, the tip of their finger never hits your tongue, does it? They must have great concentration to do that by the way; hummingbirds and aircraft refuellers are only the haypenny place compared to them.

As long as that was all it was, having to crush the life out of him against the kitchen doorjam everytime he wanted a cup of tea, I didn't mind. It was when he started asking me if I wanted breakfast in bed on Saturday - merciful hour! - that I thought not on your nelly, never mix business with religion or whatever.

I happened to mention it to my probation officer, Chantal.

'What would you do if your employer brought you breakfast in bed,' I asked her, 'wearing nothing but silk pyjamas and a cravat?'

'Not the Father!' she says.

'No,' says I, 'it's a hypo-whaddyacallit thingamajig.'

She tried to give me good advice, God love her, considering she was only nineteen, though I thought better of cutting up his soutane, or complaining to his employer. As far as his employer, you might as well be talking to the wall. 'The buck doesn't even slow down here,' is their motto.

I was on me own, as per usual, muggins, and the only thing I could think of was that aversion therapy. It's not only electric shocks, there's more to it than that. Like I used to love Carbody's Nutpic bars till I ate three of them in a row one day and puked me ring up. (You'll have to excuse me coarse expressions, I've an awful gob on me lately.) I'm a glutton you see, but the one thing I can't even look at now without heaving is a Nutpic bar. In fact it put me off all sweets with nuts in them, I swear to God. But I divest.

So when Lord Muck brings in my breakfast this Saturday, I drop a book down the back of the bed (the Pope's book it was, I don't really read.)

Here's me, 'I'm awfully sorry, but could you get that for me, Father?'

When he's down on his knees rootin' under the bed, I swing me legs out, one on each side of him. And I'm commando now, if you catch my drift, I like me Germaine Greer to have free fresh air at all times - y'know what I mean.

'Oh Mrs Haverty, that's very pious of you,' he's saying when he sees the white and gold cover of the Pope's book. But when he backs out from under the bed his head comes up inside me nightie.

'Father Tierney! I'm surprised at you!' says I, as if butter wouldn't melt in me mouth.

'Sorry,' he sort of squeals, but he's still under there.

'Would this be a good time to ask you about resumin' me pastoral duties?'

You could say I had him where I wanted him. I tightened me thighs around his head, and I must admit now, I did get a little carried away. You know the way you just want to squeeze a little baby, that you'd nearly squeeze the life out of it, and then you'd feel guilty. I think the question had him dumbfounded, and I was under the impression that he was trying to think of the right answer but just couldn't. How wrong can you be?

I know you're probably thinking I smothered him, but as God's me witness, you're wrong. I'm not sure if he passed out, but whatever way it took him he was never the same again. That was no bad thing, mind you. Whether he was starved of oxygen or just zombified by trauma, I don't know, all I know is he was a perfect gentleman from that day on.

I'm not sure how I got into renting the rooms out. I think it was my brother, the one with the shotgun, I mentioned earlier, after he paid me a flying visit and recommended the presbytery to some friends of his, and of course nothing would please them when they were leaving but to stuff wads of notes down me boobs. Would you get up the yard I said, I feel like one of them pole dancers.

It mushroomed from there. Seven bedrooms there were, but of course I had to keep one for meself. I moved Fr Tierney, or what was left of him I should say, into the pantry, where there was a grand broad shelf, and that freed up another room. Payment was all voluntary, but it'd do your heart good the way you'd see them calculating based on this or that hotel, and of course we Irish being generous to a fault.

I even had little flyers printed for "Retreats at the Presbytery" to try and boost the off-season business. They were a common sight in certain places around Ireland for a while.

One girl, Mabel, stayed on with me while she was looking for a job. A good girl she was, although she was English, adopted in Ireland – it's a long story – anyway, good as gold she was. She was awful pale though, and sickly. She didn't really eat, or not what I'd call eating; she was on a feed of drink, I'm nearly sure.

Fair play to you Mabel, I thought though, I've never known anyone to have as many friends in and out at all hours of the day and night. One thing about her, though she was only a little mouse, she was more than generous paying for her keep. I often thought of having a word with her about some of the unsuitable boyfriends she dragged in, shifty geezers with big cars and if I said surly, sullen so-and-sos, it'd give you an idea, but they seemed to ring her bell anyway. This is it.

She got on marvellous with Fr Tierney; she was the only one who could understand what he was saying. Then there was Zoey, another English girl, her pal who came to stay that winter, what year was it now? I forget. Well! The transformation of Fr Tierney was only a miracle.

I thought it was a record they were playing when I looked into the parlour one evening, Richard Clayderman or - what's his name – Liberace, but what was it only Fr Tierney playing the ould upright piano and Mabel dancing with a portly gentleman, a builder I'd say, and Zoey having a cuddle on the sofa with somebody I couldn't see.

This is great, I thought.

'Do you know the Walls of Limerick?' I shouted in at them, but of course they didn't get it.

'The walls of Kilburn, more likely,' they probably said. Would you go 'way.

And Zoey – exactly the same: a hundred quid every Friday. On the barrel. I'd never be able for them. I thought crikey, these English girls are good crack, and I told them to tell their frends whenever they wanted the place it was here, and soon we had all the rooms full of lovely little girls.

Fr Tierney was in seventh heaven, as long as he had a ball of malt and his pipe and a few lads and lasses for company, and him playing them all this sort of higgledy piggledy music he used to make up.

All I had to do was make sure me buckos they brought in behaved themselves, though of course I knew they were doing the bold thing upstairs in the bedrooms. I didn't come down the Liffey on the last lily pad, meself, and anyway nothing shocks you after Holloway.

The little envelopes that the volunteers collected from the faithful came in handy too, now that I had the run of the place. I was able to install a jacuzzi and a steam room, on a two for the price of one offer from Valentine's Leisure Factors. Life couldn't have been any better, but was I happy? Something was missing, something with a handbrake in the trouser area, and arms like diggers. Do you follow me?

I knew it, I knew something was going to happen, there were that many weirdos always playing with their cigarette lighters and bits of tinfoil, it was only going to be a matter of time till there was a disaster. I don't know if they ever found the cause of the fire – useless! Luckily I had a few bob in the building society to tide me over, and thanks be God and his holy mother I'd had the sense to insure the place.

You can't dwell on it too much, it'd do your head in, especially if you thought about all the beautiful young girls and poor old Fr Tierney, padlocked in the pantry. (They could be very cruel those same lassies when I wasn't there to keep an eye on them.) I mean I'd only gone down to the Tangiers grill for a one-and-one with mushy peas, because I didn't feel like cooking that night, and when I came back the whole place was burned to a frazzle and the fire brigades were hosing it down.

Thanks be to jazes, before dawn when the firemen left I was able to get me papers and things out of the fireproof safe. It had done its job, though it was black as the hobs of Hell, and so was I after opening it.

I thought somebody would quiz me about the fire, it being on the telly and all, but seemingly they didn't even know I existed.

I went into a cheap B&B, just picked one at random. I know I must've looked a fright with me chimneysweep face and hands, manky ould pink crimplene slacks, Aran cardigan, and me plastic bag full of papers. I could see the hatchet-faced cow at the desk doing a double-take when she looked at me.

'I'm sorry we've no rooms available.'

Now there was a sign outside that said, 'Rooms Available', y'know.

'The sign is out-of-date,' says she.

I was going to give her a piece of me mind, but I couldn't be arsed, so I spit on a tissue, cleaned me face with it, got a taxi and checked into the feckin Four Seasons instead. I'd had enough for one day. I didn't know if I had enough cash to pay them, but I was good for it, and in anyway I wasn't going to let that stop me.

On the way I asked the cabbie to stop outside Kwality Wines in the High Road and got meself a bottle of Baileys and a packet of kettle chips, balsamic vinegar and crushed pepper flavour, and a tub of Ben & Jerry's Cherry Garcia, and I thought I might as well be hung for a sheep as a lamb and got meself a tub of Haagen Dazs Strawberry Cheesecake ice cream, and a box of Irish Roses. Unless you look after yourself, nobody else will.

You'll never guess who I met going up in the lift at the Four Seasons, when I was going to my room. Lionel Cohen, y'know – music to slit your wrists by. He looked that miserable, I thought I'd ask him for a midnight feast in my room, with the ice cream just reaching the right temperature and all, and then I thought, sure he has the mini-bar and room service, so I just said, "Did you bring your ould banjo with you?' Well, the imper'ent get didn't even have the courtesy to answer me. It occurred to me after, when I was lying in bed, I should've said 'Ice cream, Cohen?' – but you never think of these witty remarks till it's too late.

I left the impression of poor old Fr Tierney's visa card. It only had his initials on, and I gave the name Giselle Tierney. This was before chip & pin – and I practiced his signature before going out in the morning, for a ramble through Hyde Park with the bulging, horsey people lolloping around and their horses dunging up the trail there.

I got meself a new outfit with the card in Horrids, before breakfast. I passed by about 50 restaurants till I found a self-service one in there – I hate all that asking Alphonse to get it and waiting half an hour. Jaze, life's a bit too short, so I barged in and scooped up a few Danish and blah blah and I know you're not going to believe it, but there on the cover of the Morning Bugle, "Lionel Cohen found dead in London hotel." I felt terrible, because I thought I should've offered the Cherry Garcia, and all, but anyway it was lovely, though I'd a head like a buffalo on me in the morning, and the aftertaste – stop! I'm dry retching just at the thought.

Who should walk in only that little Arab oulfella that owns the place, does be on the Graham Norton show and all, nearly married the Queen – a jolly little man – and doesn't he come and sit at me table.

'I see you have a good eye,' says he.

I'm thinking he has a feckin nerve drawing attention to me good eye, as if to say I notice you have one lazy eye.

Then he says, 'Max Mara.'

'Carmencita,' says I. 'I thought you were that Mustafa Al Yamani. You're the spit of him.'

'Well, suits you anyway,' says he.

What a dozy omadaun I was. Wasn't it the Max Mara suit I'd put on he was talking about. I'd stuck th'oul' crimplene kak in a bin. So trying to be cute I commented on his jacket.

'Armani, is it?'

'Yamani,' he says.

Here's me going to say, 'I love Armani - massive, isn't it?' when a stubbly-headed ibek slides in between the tables, like an accident looking for somewhere to happen, with a feckin big camera and saddled up like a mule with leather bags, and starts snapping us. *Schluck, schluck, schluck...*

Out of nowhere, a two-seater, brick shithouse of a character appears and starts shoving the stubbly-headed geezer out of the caf, as he's shouting back at me, 'What's your name, Madam?'

'Carmencita Haverty,' says I.

'Don't tell him,' says the little Arab, but it's too late.

'Very fucking good,' says he. 'You be in the fucking papers tomorrow.'

'Here,' says I, 'you might be a big knob in the Casbah, but don't you start fucking me, you oily-haired bag of shite.'

Oh I can give as good as I get. I don't care whether you're Lionel Cohen or Mustafa Yamani or Abdul Abulbul Amir, the least you can do is keep a civil tongue in your head.

At the same time, doesn't that cameraman slither out of the bouncer's grip, and whatever way he was squeezing his arm the strap of the big feckin Hasselblad or whatever it was came over in arc like a Roman thingummy and bashed Mustafa Al Yamani's head in. Crazy horses!

Well it wasn't just depressing it was bloody inconvenient. It was all over the news and if the black enamel bollocks had even survived for a week or two it'd all have blown over, but no such luck. And that's how I landed back in HMP Holloway, not that it's any great hardship, I'm well used to the bull dykes and the sadists, they give me a wide berth. They call me Superglue Sue. They can't menace you with their boobs stuck to their bedposts.

It was only a fecky little thing, I'd forgotten to report to me probation officer (Chantal) for a couple of weeks, with all the excitement – I can be a dopey cow – and I got greedy too and signed up with Max Clapton for a kiss and tell story about ould Mustafa, all codswallop of course, and as a result they tracked me down. In anyway it's only like a rest cure here, and I'll be out in time for the summer, so look out for me ad in Time Out. 'Time Out' is right. Jaze.

Amy Muldoon

Secret Messages from the Amazing Ghost Boy

There are hidden messages everywhere. We see them and pass by, not taking the time to think, to decipher the codes. Even when we write, what is being said is not always in the black type, but in the pale and empty space between, written in invisible ink.

I wonder how many messages, how many stories I have lost in my life, because I did not see them.

I am looking for them, now. I find them on crumpled bits of blue lined paper, in empty soda bottles, on laundry piles, scribbled in the margins of phonebooks. One message was written in invisible ink on the cap of a beer bottle, discovered hidden beneath a couch cushion. To the untrained eye, it appeared to be the cap of a beer bottle.

I know better.

I have received messages from The Amazing Ghost Boy, Super Hero Extraordinaire, Abuser of Garden Gnomes, Defender of Absurdity.

He is invisible now, appearing to me only in lightning moments; a song, a breath, a movement seen out of the corner of my eye. He passed me once in the hall, walking swiftly past, his hands shoved deep into his pockets, dark hair falling over one eye, brow furrowed, and eyes far away, as if he, too, was deep in thought.

He did not look happy.

I wonder why he didn't look at me as he passed. Perhaps he is growing used to being unseen.

He became invisible without warning, on a summer evening. His new form was granted to him by a drunk man who should not have been driving. Until the drunken man chose to drive, the Amazing Ghost Boy was an ordinary extraordinary boy, in the process of becoming a young man.

Now, the young man is gone.

For a very long time, I didn't see the messages he left behind. My eyes were disabled. I could not see around the pain. There was shattered glass in my throat. My voice was gone. My words left me. I did not like the sounds that came out of my mouth. They were ugly, wounded noises. When I wrote, I saw the sounds on paper.

The first secret messages were hidden in an ordinary black backpack. They were well disguised. For many weeks, the ordinary backpack was something called evidence. Locked away, guarded by men with guns, hidden from me.

I signed for it at the police station. I wrote my name. I wrote the word mother.

I closed my eyes when they handed the pack to me. I was afraid to look. I was afraid it would be wounded. I was afraid it would be damaged. I was afraid, most of all, that I might see blood. I did not think the word, because it hurt. Thinking it not thinking it.

I didn't breathe. Just felt the fabric under my fingers. Rough nylon, suede straps, cold metal fasteners and buckles. It is not just a backpack. It's part of him, going everywhere, witness to marvelous misadventures. Witness to the last day. I can't open my eyes. I want this part of him. I don't want to see the story the backpack has to tell. The fluorescent lights in the police station are very loud.

I only open my eyes when my husband whispers to me. He says, "It's all right." He means the backpack. He means that he can hear my thoughts, that it is safe to look.

There is only one small rip on it, the fabric coming apart from the shoulder strap. There is a smear of white paint. Very innocent looking, white against black. The truck was white. The fence was white. I don't think about white paint anymore.

We don't speak on the way home. The sun is bright, but we don't feel the sun. I hold the backpack against my heart, like a new mother bringing her baby home for the first time. It is an odd, ugly, reflection of a day nineteen years before. But now, we are taking home an ending.

We sit on the living room floor to open it. We sit in a circle, like pilgrims who are viewing a holy relic. We want answers. We want messages. We want mysteries revealed.

Our daughter sits apart, her holy innocent face still and white. The sun makes a halo behind her, and dust dances around her stillness. She is afraid when I open the backpack. She understands that we are letting her brother loose in the room. I want to. I don't want to.

I want to leave the backpack there in the middle of the floor forever, and pretend that he has just flung it down and gone into the other room. I have seen this sight a million times. I have complained about it. Now, I want it back. Annoying boy, never putting anything away.

This is the first lesson I learn, the first of the Hidden Messages: Ordinary things are precious, and we don't see them.

My eyes are burning still, but they are open.

The fabric is torn. We can mend it, but the rip will still show. It can't be restored. All the frayed ends, that were once woven together.

These are the mysterious messages of the backpack, revealed:

A case of CDs. The names of the bands mean things. Bad Religion, Green Day, Humping Rhinos, Dead Kennedys. I whisper the words like an incantation, and another secret message is revealed. The secret message is this: you must do what makes you happy, even if it is not profitable, or smiled upon. If you need to stand on a stage and make angry noises, do so. People will admire your screams. Show your bare ass to the audience. Write angry words, and sing them.

There are library books. I hold them, open them, touch my fingers to the pages where his fingers have been, waiting for messages. The Hobbit. The Godfather. Slaughterhouse 5.

In *Slaughterhouse 5*, people don't die, really. Time is all happening all at once. You are born you are getting married you are going to school you are dying all at the same time. Whenever there is a death in the story (and there are many) Kurt Vonnegut says: So it goes.

This is another secret message. The books say: you thought I was not listening to you, but I was. I am not as unlike you as I pretended to be. Part of you is part of me. We reflect each other, always. An occasional eclipse is nothing.

I never return the books to the library. I put them back into the backpack. They are his, they are part of a sacred time capsule.

There is a notebook, with very poor and scrawling writing decorating the blue lines. His words, his thoughts. Parts of songs that will never be written, phone numbers of friends that he will never call. This is treasure. The secret codes are wild and many. It will take me many months to understand all of them, if I ever do.

On one page, he has written a to-do list. This is what it says:

1: call casey, and see if he needs a roommate.

2: call those bastards at seafirst bank. give them money.
3: pick up paycheck
4: call mom. Ask how to make red sauce.
5: turn into batman. Take over gotham city and save the world.

These are the magic words. The Amazing Ghost boy is set free, he is dancing around us in the living room, and a cold wind touches our faces as he passes by. He sits in his favorite chair, and smiles, pleased with us, pleased with himself. We laugh, recognizing him, and touch the dark blue ink that is him, an eternal scrawl on the page, and there is a dark and sorrowful sound in our laughter. So it goes.

This is the secret message:

There is a young man, walking down the street on a summer night. The sun is just setting. His hands are deep in his pockets, and he is singing to himself, because he likes to sing to himself, and he is happy. People who know him laugh as they drive by, because he is handsome and funny, and they know that if they spoke to him, he would say something absurd and wonderful.

He is going home to eat manicotti, with extra red sauce on the side. When he eats, he looks at his plate with great love and admiration. Sometimes, he looks from the plate to his mother, and his expression is much the same. He understands that sometimes, food is not just food.

He will invite his friends over, because he loves his friends, and he likes to share his food that is not just food. They will eat together, and when they have finished, they will stand in the kitchen and eat what is left in the pan, and laugh, and, make plans for the night, or for the year. Sometimes, his friends flirt with his sister. He will stand where they can't see him, and make faces of great disgust and horror. When he thinks nobody is watching, he looks at his sister, and there will be a look on his face that is equally puzzled and proud, as if he doesn't understand how she became beautiful.

He and his father will trade loud insults. This is how they say, I love you, without ever saying so. They say, you silly bastard, you willy woofter, you mindless son of a bitch, you butt cheese connoisseur, you great tit.

He is going home, walking past his grandmother's house, past neighbor's houses where he has, in the past, rearranged the garden gnomes into obscene positions. He has roller skated and skateboarded down this street, he has waited on the corner, hidden beneath a cardboard box, waiting to startle a passer by. He has run down this street in a superman suit, he has performed amazing dances with garden hoses on the lawns.

His eyes are dark and happy and content, looking far away, deep in thought. He is thinking of the things he will do.

He does none of them.

Instead, he flies into the heart of the sun, through lightning brilliant white heat. He explodes through the other side, and emerges as shards of light, thrown across the darkness. He is a constellation.

When I look at the stars, I whisper his name.

He leaves behind an ordinary black backpack. He leaves me, in a pale and empty space, searching for secret messages.

Zink Poe

Merging on Highways with Orange Barrels

This insistence, this heaviness is suffocating, like a large Persian cat upon my chest but with no purr, no softness, no comfort whatsoever. I turn over, gathering no sleep and dreams confined once again to glass boxes scattered in the few rooms I occupy. Classical music weaves its way around my ears, nibbling and makes me angry. Stupid music. Who told it to do that? Tapestry of sound and I can't afford to get caught in it this morning.

Tumbling out of bed and almost landing on the floor like a clean load of laundry, I shake my head to rattle the cage. Fuzzy images fall out and land with a finality on the carpet. Where did it go? *Where did what go,* the far-away forgotten sort of related entity attached to me. Me. Where did I go?

Last night I was someone else.

Moody and reserved, quiet and slow slide of the eyes, the upturned lashes and the tiny smile peeking from the corner. The unexplored, the Sahara, the Siberian, the vast emptiness of the breeze near the ocean. I dive in and out with abandon, frolicking...I am a dolphin. Slippery and wet and hard to hold.

Jeff the Doorman looked at me in a weird way, his thick black brows gathered like nervous birds waiting for their food. I had no food. I sighed and moved slowly past him, thinking if only I can make it to the door, I won't scream. Maybe I'll cry once inside. This outfit didn't work for me, either. But the air was cool and revived me, and suddenly I was sharp as an edge of jagged glass, ready to cut into the first face I'd see. And there he was, alone, drinking. Alone and drinking is par for the course around here and hey, take your pick. I chose him because he was oblivious and still. No motion came from him except the slow raise of the tumbler to his lips. Then he would sip even more slowly and then slowly lower the tumbler. A well-oiled soul. I needed to make his acquaintance.

So in my sneaky little way, I silently lowered my self, which already felt too heavy, into the leather barstool and looked him over. I motioned for the bartender and he took my order for a white russian. These little gems tasted like chocolate milk and made me feel a bit like a school kid smoking a cigarette in the bathroom during recess. Naughty but not evil. Evil was reserved for the darker moments in the night when all one had was a wish and no exits. The guy took a quick look at me and then began his well-oiled motion all over again.

"Hi." He looked as though I woke him from a mediocre dream. I gave him a little smile and did my own well-oiled motion.

"Um. Yeah. Hi." He looked straight ahead.

"So, who do you want to kill tonight?" I thought shock treatment would work.

"Whaaa'???" His eyes suddenly were open full moons with a shadow of shooting stars imminent. Hmmm. Maybe I hit something.

"How did you know?" I gave one those little wise smiles that I practiced for years until it fit. Yes, I knew these types of nights well.

"Well, you had this resolved look on your face. All you need is a gun."

He snorted. "A gun, yes. That would do. That would do well. But it's too late and she's long gone. Thanks though, for the cheer." He swallowed the last of his drink and then turned to face me. "So, do you want to kill anyone?"

"Hmm. Good question. I'd like to kill my curiosity." Now I stared ahead and took a slow sip.

"Oh really? That sounds difficult."

"Yes, My curiosity is a very elusive animal. Hard to nail down. I'm tired though, it keeps whipping me around all the garbage cans at night and then I return home, smelling of rotten food and sour milk. I don't like it."

"Well, get drunk then." He looked like he had discovered the cure for cancer.

"That doesn't work. It only makes it more voracious, more moral. It's a self-righteous little bastard, this curiosity. I want to ride roller coasters until I die. This is a good thought." I took an ice cube and swirled it in my mouth, deliberately allowing it to rest on my metal fillings and feeling the shockwave rotate through my skull.

"I wonder what Einstein did to take a break." I mumbled.

"Oh? So you're an Einstein?" He looked amused.

"No."

"A Silverstein?"

"No."

"A gypsy?"

"At times. Give me your money." He laughed but I was serious.

He ordered another drink and another and then I did too until we both were drunk, talking gibberish and understanding one another perfectly. He told me he needed to leave so that he could work on his sermon for the next day. I nodded understandingly and left like a ghost. Jeff the Doorman smiled at me and said something that he thought was funny but I didn't get.

I drove onto the highway, empty as the lanes next to me. Occasional orange barrels lined the side, ready to protect the new road, proclaiming progress. I envied their unity.

Where was I? Oh yes, getting up. Maybe a good hot shower will help. That and a new outfit.

Kenji Siratori

Experiment

The sun of ADAM that splits a cell the artificial love of the clone the embryo of catastroph who the chromosome of the heat of myself goes up in flames the cadaver city where records the brain of the ant of the drug mechanism_being eroded the malice of the interior of the womb that thinks about the zero of the inorganic substance reproduction area cell of DNA=channel clone-TOKAGE that was cut off to the cold-blooded desire of the world=womb=cell that contaminates clonic soul of the murder of ADAM to the crime of yellow ADAM of the artificial paradise that the season of the treachery of the chromosome of myself charms her of the zero-level of an embryo the pupil of the zero of the machine mechanism of myself the body the interference of the clone_overturning I forget the love of her clone as the machine of an embryo is doing the zero gravity_soul of myself suck blood so with the cruel womb cell of yourself and coexists

Artificial sun of the centipede that the high speed body of an ant crashes to the digital=vampire of the brain of anti-faust to the apoptosis placenta universe of the fatalities that the consciousness of the disillusionment of myself that the human body gimmick of ADAM speeds up play strange the devilish homicide of the cyber space of an embryo so exposes the internal organ of ADAM and era is respired it is penetrated the love of the clone the speed of the limit of a cell war to the eyes of the drug embryo of the immortality that resuscitate the scribe=zone of the soul of myself that is cloning the nerve fiber of the nightmare of the larva machine in the human immunodeficiency virus system outer space of the cyber embryo where mills the hearing organ of myself and induce the brain of the zero of the fatalities and do the abnormal living body of the zero of ADAM+myself interference in the cold desert of the apocalypse

The speed of the zero of the embryo that the blue murderous intention of the sky of fatalities awoke to the apoptosis block of the cruel womb cells of ADAM which the druggy consciousness of myself changes to the catastrophic murder machine of the artificial sun cuts the storage of her murder and tore! Miracle of the immortality of the embryo is guided to the drug mechanism to clone-dive of the topological love that the cell of the zero of myself that the larva machine of the disillusionment of myself that the sea of the eve_gene does the level of the zero of the cadaver city that does short to the nest form replicant brains of the spider of yourself desire be flooded commit suicide toward the horizon of DNA so octave of murder to

chaos gene=TV of myself that explodes and invade the
digital=vamp body fluid of ADAM with the clonic ruin
of the artificial sun like the boundless end of the
machine of yourself that was projected

Dean Strom

Down with the Count

Americans have become an ugly race. The women obese. It wasn't like this when I was young in the 1940s. Nor when I was still young in the 1970's. Fat girls were the exception in the 40s and 70s. Today the svelte one is. Now by the time a girl reaches adolescence and desires to be sexy and sport an exposed midriff it's already rolls she is flaunting. Her ass is, in the best cases, merely flabby. And plenty are gargantuan. And goddamn if they aren't mindlessly flaunting it anyway. I don't think they realise they're fat because they're all goddamn fat. I feel for today's boys. Some of them are obese as well but fewer. Boys might still be more active. I'm sure they're just as horny and forced to compete in the pool of fat blabby girls.

I'm a vampire and have been since 1950. Haven't aged a day to look at. I've changed in fashion and have lived fully in all of them. I'm not particularly nostalgic for anything except for the days when women weren't all fat. Now here's the deal. I haven't sucked any fresh blood for three years relying on my stock of refrigerated plasma but I've been getting kind of thirsty lately so I whisk into a small town and step into a bar. I don't know what you know about vampires but this is one bat that mixes the ethanol. The life of your next party might just be a drunken vampire.

I order a bloody mary because that never gets old. You're supposed to think a band is playing but it's really just a guy on a guitar strumming some chords, a female singer, and a laptop computer plugged into an amp. There are about one hundred people. Roughly half are women. That makes 50 women. And out of that 50 five of them are not fat. Plenty are perfectly obese. I spot an empty area with a stool and a place to set my drink. Directly in front are a few tables and the dance floor and a little to the right the "band." One of these five thin women tonight will receive my dispensation.

#1 is clearly in love with her damn little self. Her little damned self as I am about to make it. She bounces and glistens and dampens the dance floor. Her lithe and nimble body celebrates because tonight she is the beautifullest girl. And her neck... My teeth will grow quick and sink deep into this neck. It's long and curvy and her head lollygags above it. Her blonde hair will caress my face with the soft breezes of the cradle while I siphon deep and long from her jugular.

Or maybe the tall one. Choice #2 has short blonde hair but the underside is brown and it is slightly turned up at the ends. She has a large wingspan and on each of her biceps is a tattoo. On her right bicep is a long depiction of a nude Statue of Liberty. On the left bicep is that butterfly that gets around so much. I haven't seen her dance yet. She has passed by twice on her way to the restroom and is seated somewhat behind me to my right. Easy pickings.

Sitting close to the stage is a very thin girl. She's relaxed, animated, and friendly, and sure to be particularly satisfying. I will take her from behind and she will fold comfortably beneath and all but disappear. It will be sweet and quick but the aftertaste might remain for a couple of weeks. She'll purr as she goes softly.

#4 is dark and booby by the bar, surrounded by boys. The only one wearing a skirt. The others favoring small tops and jeans. The only one to have yet exposed her eyes to me and she's struggling to not look.

I can't get a good look at the fifth one. As I turn around I still cannot see her face. A good postured figure.

The waitress is here with my second drink, a double. As she is leaving something fills the area like a stifling shadow of armpit and I focus in to realise it is two fat broads who are occluding the space in an ever crowdening bar. I catch a partial glance at option girl 5 who passes behind eclipsed by the enormous asses. She moves out of sight entirely in the direction of the restrooms. I softly emit a high frequency hum designed to be a vague disturbance in order to cause them to move. They continue to blobber oblivious. Ooomph. I'm a little shaky. I'm out of shape. When running good I can knock a cow over.

All right. So I've been spending more time straightening my pants while watching reality t.v. lately than actively following my calling. But I haven't lost it. Just order another drink and get into it a little. Relax. As the guitarist plays or pretends to play chords from another Steve Miller song option 5 flashes on my cornea briefly again and is gone. A sudden flash of anger uses me. An experience that harkens back. Way back to prevampire. I am never angry. Never. This is remarkable. The two space hogs hurry away.

I can see the dance floor once again and see pigs dance. Stop it. Disappear. Not the whole you. Just most of you. Dissolve into something slender. Goddamn ugly stupid pigs, lose some blob. I suppose this anger is not a huge step beyond amused disgust. I will piss and walk to the restroom, into a stall, unzip and reach in. My penis has withdrawn. It is hardly a nub. I can barely point but manage to pee. And return to my drink.

Choice 1 is dancing with a different guy and it's his hands all over her now.

Number four. Queen of the bar. She's got world-class legs and will always have that memory. Always, that is, lasting a short time while in denial, then becoming a memory of the memory and in a few more short years she'll be dead. Or I could just take her tonight in her prime. Does she deserve me or should I let her rot in time?

Number three seems even thinner than a few minutes ago. Something becoming apparent. She is sad. Her happy making is for the benefit of being social. She carries her sadness with grace. She is a wise and beautiful girl. I think it will be this one. I run my eyes over her body and I can feel each tender curve. I return to the restroom. My cock is back and is big in my hand.

Now to draw her to me. And after we will take a walk and I will administer the joy. But I do not understand. As I focus on her she gets thinner. And thinner. Fading. She is no longer there. The others at her table carry on without seeming to notice. Look away and look again and she is still not there. She's gone. And something is wrong.

Numbers 1 and 4 are still there. 2 is okay. I turn around and see #5. The waitress arrives with another drink and asks if I'm okay. I've never been asked this before. I'm not sure but yeah I'll be fine. She tries to think of more to say but I'll not be waiting around for any waitress to get off tonight and I dismiss her. And then the plan becomes clear.

Number 5 walks into view and past and this time I see her. Though she doesn't look toward me this is the one. She is that right mix of attitude and tit. Her hair falls over one eye Veronica Lake style. She wears dark framed glasses. Braless nipples are clearly upturned. She has the perfect athletic gait but feminine. If I was the marrying type... Chuckle.

I'm not going to waste anymore time tonight on the dance. When she comes back across the room I'll hit her with something that'll knock her out. I need to get one under my belt. Here she comes. Her jaw is set and she traverses the space decidedly and I hit her with it. I shoot all my stuff at her and she doesn't bend. No glance. Not even a blink. And removes herself once again from my view.

The room is spinning and I grab hold of myself and slap some superior being back into me. I don't quite know what has happened here but I'm not going to act like some panicky human. I wonder if there's something funny with my supply of plasma. It might not have been the best idea to have relied on only that for so long. I'll get myself back into shape. Let's see. #3 is still gone. #2, the tattoo girl, has been trying to get my attention but she is the least interesting. She's the kind of girl you expect to fall for a vampire and I have had hundreds of those. But she might have to do. I'll have to go talk to her, I suppose, because I'm feeling too tired to perform with a concerted effort. Once I begin to talk she'll follow me outside. Then we can do the deed and I can get out of here. But there are going to have to be some changes. Perhaps a move to a better climate. Maybe Mexico City. Or Rio de Janiero. Perhaps take up cards again and suckering millionaires. Tease countesses in Monaco. A little classic vampirism. I've been stuck in Mobile too long, Bob. As vampires go I've been acting like the trailer variety. I've had my slump now and I'll get back in the fly. Let's get this night over with.

I plant my drink and walk up to #2 and direct her eyes to me. I lower my chin and the words basso-rumble off my tongue, "You want to dance?"

"No thank you."

At first I don't hear. I am floating my turn toward the dance floor with my hand on her elbow. I am in full Fred Astaire. Then it hits me what she has said. I have heard of this and seen this done to poor slob mortal men and observed near pathetic displays of a man's crushed legitimacy. But I have never heard these words before directed toward me. I have never suffered anything like this moment and I'll take the stake through my heart that you all think a vampire is vulnerable to.

"I said no."

I almost fall but stumble back to my stool while mocking eyes expose my nakedness and tiny bat heart. I'll slaughter Dorothy's little dog Toto with my bare hands. This is not how a vampire should act. I hit my head against the corner of the wall as I slip off my seat trying to get into it. It doesn't hurt but adds to the spectacle. I sit perfectly still.

Finally I long-swallow the rest of my drink right as the waitress walks up. I peer at her not knowing what to expect. But she returns my look with concern and I am reassured.

"Are you alright?"

"Uh no. I'd like another please."

"Sure."

And she brings another.

#5, who I am pretty sure has not seen what has transpired from where she has been sitting, now walks into my area with some other blob girl. They stand around and I begin throwing everything at her wildly. Turn and look at me. Come on. Please. Just a glance. I won't even try to bite. Just acknowledge me.

Nothing.

A guy asks her to dance. They dance. I watch her. The dance ends without a glimmer of an indication that I exist. And I am not sure that I do. I look to the mirror on the wall on the other side of the dance floor. I don't know if that's my reflection or not. She continues to talk to her friend for a bit then returns to her table. But this time it is pointedly that she doesn't glance at me. She has looked at every sector and subsector of her view circle except the precise area where I sit.

I'm not going to just sit and take this. I get up to walk past her. Again not even a nibble. I continue to walk and almost walk right out the door but return, no look, to my drink and finish it. I'm feeling that sort of drunkeness that is vaguely in my prememory and swirl around in my stool to stare at her table. I've given up all thought about numbers 1 and 4. What is wrong? Damn you, bitch. Can't you see me here?

"One more, please."

"Are you sure you're okay?"

"Yes. I'm fine. Fine. What? Come on. Oh yeah. I have something on my mind. But it's nothing. Really. One more but make it a shot of Patrone."

"Well... okay."

Yeah. Okay. Ferchrissakes. Bring me the fucking drink. This is a goddamn bar, isn't it? Maybe I'll need to wait for the waitress to get off. No. Fuck that and fuck this version of vampire middle age. Do I need to start taking the bus? Will I incinerate in place? What kind of...? Oh come on. Stop it, you sniveling fangbastard. You exist long enough you see everything. Pull yourself together, you used up bag of soiled tuxedo. What the... The shot is here. Tastes like shit but it's down. Gawd. Now I'm having trouble focusing. What's next? Puking?

I have to get out. "Get some air." What a strange concept. But it seems true. Something seems true in all this false. If I can just pull myself up. Okay. I'm leaving. I'm really leaving. I will just crawl back to my coffin and get some rest. I'll sleep for a week and forget about all this. When I come out next time I will have a plan and my old self back again. Just sleep this fiasco off.

As I blearily stumble forth I can wavily glimpse numbers 1 and 4 still at their places and bitchily so. I'm not sure I even like the taste of women anymore. You can see where mankind has gone astray when you watch women growing fat and rejecting the tenets of motherhood by shmoozing haphazardly their children's fathers. It's really women who despise the human race. It's not vampires. We vampires have a soft spot for humans. Nostalgia become manifest. Actualized. When you're being done, girls, and I'm sucking the last of your few pints of love, because I don't stop at a sip, just remember it is yourself you fear while me you pin it on.

I draw up all my strength and feign savoir vivre and turn to the exit passing what was once prospect #5 and I'm too drunk to do anything about it anyway and it's obvious I am leaving and now she looks. Now she takes the time to look. What, bitch? Do me the courtesy of ignoring me on the way out as well. It must be pretty lonely at the top of your come and get me because it's been damn succulent as the knight in waiting pose at your toes. Now you're just another glance away. So glance away and let me forget you.

Out the door the air isn't fresh as far as I can tell but it is a change and will lift my wings and I'll be away. But not yet. Damn it. This isn't over. It used to be, in the early days, I would surprise them along the Seine from behind. I'll hide and wait for maybe even a fat one. Now, where is the best dark corner? Oh ye, the desirable, the figment of my yesteryear, forgive me my disgust or don't, it's too late now, I'm nothing but the horse ear flicking when it must.

Dean Strom

The Death of Damn Henry

The Last Act of a Five Act Play Encompassing Many Scenes

Somewhere deep within the castle.

Damn Henry: I DON'T KNOW WHAT. AAAAAAAAHHH. Fuck. Fuck. Fuck. Fuck. There were guys... Guys who could count... Yeti... need more peanuts... them damn stupid peasants... Write, you fuckers. Write. Now where did that thought go? I saw it there a minute ago. Put this down... hmmm. Biographers. The bunny is back. The rabbit. Where is Dark Glasses? Shnark. There you are. Come here.

Shnark: Yes, Sir?

Damn Henry: Where's Dark?

Shnark: uh Sir. I uh um don't um know. Sir.

The Death of Damn Henry

Damn Henry: What the hell has been going on? The bunny, Shnark. I want the bunny. Pipobab. Bring me Pipobab.

Shnark: uh The bunny. Yes Sir. The bunny.

Damn Henry: And hurry or I'll have him boing on your head. You hear me, Shnark? What have you done for me lately? Get fucking going.

Shnark: uh uh uh Yes sir. (The bunny; the bunny. Fuck you, sir. Yeah, I'll get you the bunny, Damn Henry Gold. I'll get him for you.)

Pink Zoe and Yeti taking a walk.

Pink Zoe: Oh look, Yeti. Aren't those pretty women? I think women are pretty. I really like women. We should get us some women, Yeti.

Yeti: Arrrgh. Hmmm.

Pink Zoe: Let's slide down the waterslide into the lake again. That's what we should do. When I was sliding down the water slide the other day I was thinking about cherry cobler. Let's have dessert. You eat one of those people over there. I would never wear a nose ring. Do you have any tattoos?

Yeti: Errrgh Hhhuh.

Pink Zoe: You do? Can I see them?

Enter Dark Glasses

Dark Glasses: Yeti! Oh, ma'am. How are you, ma'am? You're looking splendid today.

Pink Zoe: Why thank you, Dark. Did you see those beautiful women on the road? Are they still there?

Dark Glasses: I saw them, Your Highness. But next to you they're scrub brush.

Pink Zoe: They are still there?

Dark Glasses: I believe they are.

Pink Zoe: I must run. Bye, Yeti. Bye, Dark.

Dark Glasses: Be careful, Miss.
(To guards) Clark. Baskins. Follow her and keep the usual distance.
(To Yeti) Look. We gotta talk.

Yeti: Taaaawk. Urrrrr. Hmmmmm. Ah. Hmm.

Dark Glasses: Yeti, you and I have been friends a long time. I was there when you ate your first baby.

Yeti: Arrrgh. Yowl errrr homm.

Enter Sean

Sean: Hey guys. What are we drinking?

Yeti: Arrrrrrrrrgh.

Dark Glasses: Freeze! Oh, it's you. I've got some potato vodka. Here. I saw Sasha back over there. Take the bottle.

Sean: Okay. You two are busy.

Dark Glasses: I'm still on the clock but I'll be off soon.

Sean leaves happily, bottle in hand

Yeti: Arrrrrrrrrrrrrrrrrrrrrrrmmmmmmmmmmmmuuuuuu uuhhhhhhhnnnnnnnnnnuuuuuuuuunnnnnnnnnnngggggg gggggg.   Daaaaaaaaaaammmmmmnnnnn Heeeeeeeeeeennnnnnnnnnnnnnn errrrrrrrrrrrr. Crazy?

Dark Glasses: Afraid so. Lost it completely. What's the doctor calling it? MPD.

Yeti: Arrrrrrrgh. Saaaaaadd hmnmmmmmmph ii ah.

Dark Glasses: We gotta think about our future, you and I. Do you hear what I'm saying?

Yeti: Fuuuuuuuuu fooooooo er ahhhhhhh errrrrrrrrr eat.

Dark Glasses: Go get yourself a meal and we'll talk later.

Damn Henry is walking along the parapet with Nardo Flesheater

Nardo: So, as I understand it, you want me to say buy more prescription drugs?

Damn Henry: Yes.   No.   Goddamnit.   It's nonprescription drugs. Where is that fucking bunny?

Nardo: What?

Damn Henry: The fucking bunny. Look. No. Never mind. No. Don't tell them that. Or tell them that. Nardo, just tell them what I said, okay?

Nardo: Okay... so... what you want me to tell them is that you give them...

Damn Henry: Hell, Nardo. The breeze. I haven't noticed the breeze in so long. The breeze will save you, Nardo...

High Priest chi chi and Scarlette are renewing their vows

chi chi: and i vow to always say things to bother you. i vow to quit sleeping crosswise on the bed and i vow that i will never never screw your dog.

Scarlette: And I vow to read all your savings.

chi chi: to spend my savings?

Scarlette: No. To read all about your saving people. Your liquid canons seep slowly into my brain.

chi chi: scarlette, it is with regret i must inform you that i am continuing this charade of idiocy. plunge this ahead is even not while clever i because become it bored is with easy this to whole do.

The Death of Damn Henry

We join Shnark who has found Pipobab

Pipobab: Boing. Boing. Chitta chitta chitta chi. I will bounce on your head if you don't buy this.

Shnark: Uh I'll take it. But um I uh want the extra potent stuff.

Pipobab: This is for Damn Henry? Yes? Boing boing boing.

Shnark: Yes. NO. uh just me. A little something um me. For me.

Pipobab: You? Boing boing boing. I didn't boing boing boing know you boing boing boing boing boing boinged. Can I interest you in some Ritalin? Boing.

Shnark: No. Just the morphine. Remember, I want the good stuff.

Pipobab: Here you go. Boing bye. Tell your kids to do lots of drugs.
Boing boing boing boing.

Shnark: (Yeah, you boing away, bunny. You're about to lose your best customer.)

Shnark mixes in rat poison and takes it to Damn Henry

Damn Henry: You found the bunny? Damn fucking about time. What did you get for me?

Snark: Here you are, sir.

Damn Henry: Just put it over there on the desk. Good Job, Shnark. Now, take this down to Flesheater. Tell him to get this out right away. It says, I'm feeling great and I plan to be your rabbit I mean leader for a very long time.

Shnark: Right away, sir. Right away.

Damn Henry pacing furiously now, alone. The room is mostly dark but lit by a low lamp partially covered by a curtain. The windows are open. The moon is full.

Damn Henry: Dunkin donuts. Creme de la creme. Broken spines. Tailor's today. Crucifictions. Batman. Dissolve Senate. Locked jaw kneeling pleaders. Need more knee pillows. Disgraceful. Lose the trumpets. Clarions and more spit valves. Border concerns. Ronald Reagan. Crushing heads more circumfrencely. Puppets. Bunnies. Pipobab. Desk. Syringe.

Meanwhile on a path to the castle

Dark Glasses: The only way to do it is to just do it. Either I shoot him or you eat him. It's for the good of the empire. I'm as loyal as the next guy but his mind is fried.

Yeti: Arrrrrgh? HuuuHHHHrrrrRRRRgagagaga.

Dark Glasses: I know you don't like the idea though to be frank I don't know why.

Yeti: Arrrrrrrrrgh. I ate Frank.

Dark Glasses: Either you do it or I do it. He would want it that way.

Yeti: Arrrrrrrgh Yes. Arrrrrrgh. You are right, Dark Glasses. You are right. You have come. Said things arrrrgh.

Dark Glasses: We'll do it right. He goes quick.

Yeti: <burp> (quick?)

Damn Henry has injected the concoction given him by Shnark

Damn   Henry: oooooeeeeeeeeeeeeeeeeeeeeeee
ooooooooooooooooooooooooooooooooooooooom
well   now,,,,,,,,   ohhhhh   okay   woh
wwwwwwwwwooooooooooooohhhhhhhhhhh what what
what what what what what? eeee iiiiiiii. ah ah ah ah ah.
whoooooooooooooooooooooooooooooooooooooo
oooo
aaaaaaaaaaaaaaaaaaaaaaaaaaaaaaaaawhoooooooooooooo
oooooooooo uh Shnark...?

Back to the path

Dark Glasses: Then it's settled. I'll get a gun into his chamber and take him out real quick. Bang bang like. Just "pop". I'll go Blam. A quick boom. Two shots. Bam bam bam. Or, just Bam bam. Just take him out quick before he knows it. Ba Ba. Like that. Just boom. Turn to him and blam blam, you know. blam blam. I'll just go boom. Just choo cho. Chaminy Bam. Boom pa pa pa pa pa pom. Boom. Uh Blam. Zam bam Boom boom boom...

Yeti: Uhuhuhuhuhuhuh Damn Henry. Arrgh.

Back to Damn Henry

Damn Henry: Shnark. Get in here. Where are you? This stuff is great.

Back to Yeti and DG

Yeti: Eat Damn Henry? Arrgh. He lets me eat. Not kill Damn Henry.

Dark Glasses: I know, Yeti. I understand. I was there, remember? I was just a kid. When Damn Henry could have killed you, he didn't. When you were exposed in that flattened canyon and were surrounded - the final battle of the territory wars. He didn't kill you. But ask yourself why. You looked up those canyon walls, I remember it as if it was yesterday, and on all sides we were there. There is nothing I could have done to stop it obviously, but I'll have you know that I wouldn't have fired my gun at you Yeti, I would have aimed it at the ground. I saw the hesitation with Damn Henry. His first instinct was to have you shot. You were already carrying what? nine or ten bullets from both sides of the battle and you had just happened upon that town for dinner. An innocent Yeti in harms way. We had 300 guns pointed at you. But Damn Henry was going to shoot you, Yeti, and it was the biggest risk he ever took not doing so but it is what has kept the empire this many years. You. You and me are the real power.

Yeti: Arrrrgh.

Yeti's soliloquy

Yeti: Eating Argh to eat yes. To not eat? Arrg? When doth pangs of hunger, rumbling drum stomach. owwwwwwwwwwwwww   wwoooooooooo   oooooo ow   Argh

AAAAAAAAAAAAAAAAaiiiiiigggggg

bloooooooooooooooom   Horse, many sheep, Argh Humans. I learned "dessert" from humans and made them mine. But Arrrgh. Hungry always. Diet. Shnark's high fat, no human diet. But giggle giggle humans. Arrrrrrrrgh I Eat Them! I Will Eat. I Am Yeti.   Arrrrrrrrrrgggghh   iiii   errrrr   gggg ************○○○○○○○○○○○○○○○(56734673

BBBBBBBBBBBBBBBBBBBVVVVVVVVVVVOOOO OOOOOOOOOOOOOOGGGGGGGGGGGGGGGG GGGGGGG HOR HOR HOR HOR HOR Ha Heem Ha Ho. Arrrrgh I Eat You. But Damn Henry. Who saved me once from death... tis nobler to not eat? Hmmmmmmmmmmmmmmm.   Haarrrrrrrrrr Hummmmmm. No tis nobler to eat. Arrrgh. To swallow the spleens and marrow of courageous knight. Damn Henry. My friend. But mad. When whole, would he that I eat him if perchance his madness were foreseen? Arrrrgh.... Or take jaws against the conspiracy.   To   eat   Dark   Glasses   Eat Arrrrrrrrrrrrrrrrrrrrrgh.   Eat AAAAAAAAAAAAAAAA.

chachachawwwwwwwwwwwwwwwww errrrrrrrrrrrrrrrrrrrrrrgh   bye   bye   bye   bye   gulp purrerrrrurrrerrrr.

Aaaaaaaaaaaaaaafffffffffffffffffffffrrrrrrrrrrrrrrrrowwwwwww wrrrrrrrrrrrrr. It gives me pause: there's the glub. For who would share the pips and porns of sacrifice? He to

feed. He fed me many poor bards. Bards AAAArrrrrrrrrrrrrrrrrgh. Bards. I will eat Myth. Arrrrgh. The insipidness of lousy poets arrrgh To eat them Yes. But who would bardels fair, to grunt and sweat under spiky fur, the bed after Eat Arrrrgh yes, the undiscovered realm of endless zebras, from whose pastures no Yetis are hungry, but then to awaken and the rumbling drum boom boom boom boom yooowwwwwwwwwwwwwwwww
hmmmmmmmmmmmmm   Arrrgh
blummmmmmmmmmmmmmble
bluummmmmmmmmmmmmmmble poom poom poom chooo arrrrrrrr dum dum dum dum yyyyyyyyyyyyyyyyy ooooooooooooooooooo   ppppppppppppppppppp paaaaaaa toooooogum hmmmmmm aaaaaaaaaaaaaaaaa Eat Eat Eat Eat Eat. This I don't know. To eat Henry, to suffer his chemistry, might surge through my veins and melt my gizzards. So horrible stomach ache yet, do I owe him a proper eating and thus the drool of resolution is puking o'er with the yellow calf's pus and temptations of meat pith and endowment, with this regard, their turrets torn apart and I eat everything in sight till there is only me. Then I will eat me. Arrrrrrrrrrrrrrrrrrrrrrrgh! I will eat Henry and then I will eat all.

Shnark realises Damn Henry's immunity has been built up to the point of rat poison having no effect. He searches around frantically for a weapon stammering uh uh uh to himself. Enter Pink Zoe.

Pink Zoe: Hi Shnark. I'm feeling great. I mean Great. Mmmmmm. Do you have the records on everbody? There's someone I'd like to look up. Just some chick... Everything okay? You seem distracted. Is Henry in? I want to tell him something.

Shnark: Oh uh ma'am. Can you come back later?

Damn Henry (from inside the chamber):   Baaaaaah! *(or something like that)*.

Pink Zoe: Oh good. He's in. See you later, Shnark.

Shnark: No. Don't... (I'll kill him with this letter opener. I'll rip him to pieces).

Enter Yeti and Dark Glasses very determined

Dark Glasses: Shnark, is he alone?

Shnark: What? Uh uh Damn... uh Henry? No. Uh Pink Zoe.

Yeti: Ahhhh.

Dark Glasses: Shit. But it can't be helped. It has to be now.

Inside the chamber

Pink Zoe: And the round breasts on that one were luscious...

Dark Glasses and Yeti burst in followed by Shnark

Damn Henry: Wha...?

Dark Glasses: Move out of the way, ma'am.

Dean Strom

Damn Henry hides behind Pink Zoe

Yeti: Aaaarrrrrrrrrrrrrrrrrrrrrrrrrrrrrrrrrrrrrrrrgh!

Pink Zoe: What is going on here? Can't we all just get along and appreciate naked women? I'll get naked for you if it will resolve this conflict. Where is Miri? Did someone shoot her? She is a weird chick. I don't even want to see her naked. But Scarlette, I'd love to see her naked. And Rose. We need new naked ones. So we can worship and adore... You boys must need it. I will strip now.

Damn Henry, Yeti, Dark Glasses, Shnark: Uh...

Damn Henry recovers first and rushes out onto the parapet

Dark Glasses: Get him, Yeti.

Damn Henry: No. I will not let you get me.

He jumps.

Damn Henry: Ha Ha Ha Ha *(all the way down)*

Crows: caw caw caw caw

Curtain drops

Dude Wallers

Bet You Can't

I was at sea again. My oldest daughter decided on a pricey liberal arts college and my youngest needed braces. Six-figure job and these kids were still too expensive. But I love my girls so I went back out – doubled up my ship time.

We were somewhere off the coast of Brazil performing a geological survey. We were looking for rocks that point to oil.

We spend weeks at sea. The job is difficult but we've all been doing it a long time. There are no women on the boat. Boredom sets in quickly. So we drink, play cards and snort coke to pass the time. When we go to shore to refuel and take on supplies we try to forget the boredom. So we drink, fuck whores, and snort coke to impress ourselves with our job. Doubling up on ship time sometimes leads to a major chemical dependency. Most of us have been in one 12-step program or another. But I'm careful now. I only snort coke on land – off the smooth tan bellies of teenage whores.

Of course, this means a lot of money spent on wasted blow because some falls off onto the sheets, some clots up with sweat, and some gets trapped in belly buttons. But it keeps me from needing it. Regimented lines whacked out on a mirror make you focus on them too much. They will own you in no time.

We were all sitting there in the galley – fifteen of us. There were three card games going. I was breaking even but this wouldn't do. I needed extra money. There was nothing I could do about the high cost of college except put off retirement a couple more years but it would sure be nice if I didn't have to give up my vices to pay for those fucking braces.

The braces cost $2500 – about 2 weekends worth of tight teenage company and the blow to pole away on it good. My baby's teeth were fucked up but I needed to be able to relax if I was going to keep working this life-sucking job. If I didn't get those teeth fixed, my brown-skinned wife would surely kick me out. Then my alcoholism would be full time. I would spend more on whores – and with the whores comes the dreaded marriage to cocaine. An affair is one thing but marriage will kill a guy.

So, like I say, we were sitting there in the galley playing cards. I was breaking even and getting bored. I suggested we do something to pick up the pace a little and I bet the dealer ten bucks that the next card he flipped would be a jack. It was a three and my ten bucks were gone. But spirits picked up. The guys saw the quick transfer of money and there was a collective "fuck poker" as the cards were dropped and side bets began to fly.

One guy pointed at another and pointed to a half-empty bottle of rum and said, "Bet you can't finish that in 5 seconds." The challenge was accepted and $100 changed hands. Guys were taking on all kinds of dares. I tried to piss in an empty bottle from 5 feet away and covered the galley floor with yellow fluid. That cost me $250. I got it back when the fool who accepted my challenge to swallow the contents of an ashtray couldn't hold it down and added to the mess on the galley floor. There was a race to see who could jerk off the fastest - $1500 changed hands. The chief geologist fished his dick out of his pants and bet no one would suck it. Someone smacked him on the head with an empty and he slumped over unconscious. Fucking scientists – we're not faggots on this boat and we sure as hell don't need to go there, not with the boredom we face.

I was down about 20 bucks but something like $6000 had passed through my fingers. The money for my baby's braces was here I just had to get hold of it. I needed a big score. I needed a bet I couldn't lose. If I did it right, I would have enough money to fix my little girl's teeth and have my cock shined for a week by two prime quality prostitutes when we got back in to Rio.

Bill was the biggest, meanest guy on the boat. Not one guy aboard was insane enough to fight him. He had everyone's respect. Once in Kazakhstan he literally tore a guy's arm off and beat him with it. The guy had grabbed the girl Bill was with and Bill got all chivalrous. We got Bill out of there before he killed the guy but things were pretty ugly. Later Bill admitted he was surprised the guy's arm came off so easy. He figured there must have been something wrong with the guy. Bill had himself checked by the ship's doc to see if he had been exposed to leprosy. "No," the doc said, "you're just a strong, mean son of a bitch Bill."

Bill was mean. He was holding most of the money in the galley. I figured there was about $4500 in his hand.

I walked up to Bill and said, "Bet you can't shit on my face." He started gurgling up a loogie. "I said SHIT Bill, not SPIT," I explained. Bill looked puzzled for a second. He looked at the wad of cash in his hand and smiled. It was clear he liked the idea of shitting on another man's face. Bill was mean, but he was respectable. If he lost he would pay without argument.

The rest of the guys had gathered around us now to see what the bet was going to be. Bill asked "How much?"

"Four thousand," I replied adding "And I'll cover all side bets too that say that Bill here can in fact shit on my face." There was an additional $2500 worth of bets. I stood to walk out of this holding six and a half thousand dollars I didn't have before. All I had to do was make sure Bill couldn't shit on my face.

Bill asked, "How are we going to do this?" I explained that I would lie down on deck and Bill would be allowed 15 minutes to squat over my face and try and shit on it. I was not allowed to move my head to dodge a falling turd. I could not use my hands in any way. I told Bill that if his dick touched me at all, I would slice the motherfucker off and quick drew my knife. Bill knew that knife; it got us all out of Kazakhstan alright. Bill looked around. The guys approved of the rules. Bill smiled again and peeled off $4000 in hundreds from his wad. He bellowed, "Are all bets covered?" And a cheer rose from the guys in the galley. Slipping on piss and puke we stepped over the fallen scientist and made our way up to the deck.

The fresh air did me good and I took in a few big lungfuls before I lay down on deck. Bill paraded around like a prizefighter. Someone gave him a cigarette to loosen his bowels. Bill said he hadn't crapped for two days – though he had to go since lunch. He removed his pants and moved his hairy ass into position about ten inches above my face. The guys were cheering, every one of them wanted to see shit land on my face. It would be good to take their money.

To shit you have to relax a little. That's what I had going for me. I had to keep a close eye on Bill's asshole. At first it was puckered up tight but the clock was ticking and Bill would have to relax soon if he was going to chase that money.

About three minutes into the event Bill's sphincter shifted a little. The knot was coming untied. I waited. I watched. Bill's butt hole was just about open…. And then it was. I blew a hard puff of air right on Bill's loose sphincter and it reflexively clinched back up. He yelled, "Arrgh!"

There were just over ten minutes left on the clock. I hoped to god I could keep Bill's sphincter reflex working. I had to be patient and not over-stimulate his asshole, otherwise the reflex would be overridden, I'd be out several thousand dollars, and 4 or 5 big processed meals would be deposited on my face.

Nine and a half minutes left on the clock – Bill's asshole unclenched again. I blew. Bill's hole puckered back up and my face was still clean. 8 minutes – same story. Bill was straining now. He was really trying to force the turd out. He wiped his brow. At 6 minutes, the turd tried to peek out again and I puffed the brown bastard back in. Bill was getting mad. I was worried his legs would fatigue from squatting and he would fall on me. Bill's back door tried to open 4 more times and I slammed it shut each time. Finally, somebody yelled, "Time!"

Bill stood up, laid the money on my chest and said, "Damn!" Then he went below to take a crap. Cheers shot up all around as I got to my feet. I collected on all bets. I was happy. My face was clean, my baby's fucked up teeth were going to be fixed, and I was going to celebrate when we got into Rio in a couple days.

Laszlo Xalieri

Falling Out

The wind was so strong it was impossible to hear what she was saying. In all honesty I was glad about this because she had been a bit shrill for some time. It was nice that she appeared to be done with the screaming.

I was certain I was hurting her by how tightly I was holding her. Hell, I was hurting myself—and she had left a few bruises and scratches of her own on *my* hide. We both put up with it for the same reasons, I guess.

The wind tore the tears from our eyes and the hair from our heads. She bit her lip and tried to choke back the hysteria. The wind interfered with taking deep breaths, which did not help.

I crushed her face to my chest, which possibly *did* help. I couldn't tell.

I was tired and wrung out. Pissed off and exhausted. I squeezed my eyes closed and concentrated on the scent of her hair. Soon I'd have no further chance to do so. Somehow I could still smell it past the wind and the streaming mucus.

"Why is this happening to us?" she (merely) shouted, in order to be heard over the fluttering roar.

"Why did you do this?"

Suddenly, it was all my fault, apparently. Like so many other things. It was so ridiculous I didn't even consider answering. The trip was completely her idea—"positive action to save our relationship," in her words. It was just my money. Typical.

I suddenly realized how sweet her body felt, pressed so firmly against mine. She was trembling with fear and rage and the inescapable chill. I wished, even though I knew I was an idiot for it, that we could have sex one last time before it was over. Stupid, stupid, impossible, stupid. But despite the ridiculous freezing cold and the unholy stress of the situation, I was getting a boner. Fucking pathetic.

My fault, my *entire* ass. This trip killed our last remaining chance to fix things. Her trip.

But it didn't seem to kill my boner. Not yet, anyway.

Denim was definitely not the right choice to be wearing outside at this altitude. Soon to be irrelevant.

We hit the rocky ground, the wreckage of the flaming airplane raining all around us.

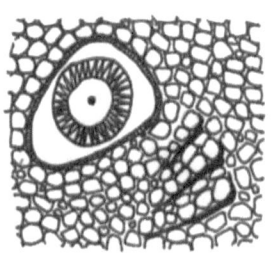

Contributors

Jeremy BeBeau dropped a Mountain Dew bottle into the East Fork of Wisconsin's Chippewa River when he was nine and has been waiting for a response ever since. He urges the eventual recoverer to send a paragraph or two about themselves to the enclosed address; his parents will be more than happy to forward it west—or whichever cardinal direction is then necessary.

J. Tyler Blue lives in Baltimore. He likes things. Many things. Even carrots. He is author of a collection of poetry and short fiction, "The Baltimore Years."

Barry Blumenfeld lives in Minneapolis. His work has appeared on the web in Exquisite Corpse, Milk, Poor Mojo's Almanac(k) and writeThis.com. He dropped out of the University of Arizona MFA program, but he had a fine time there. "Blumenfeld" is a pen name.

Sean Brijbasi collects words from the infralittoral zone where waves of poetry break onto the shore of prose. (It has been said by someone.) He is the author of two books, "One Note Symphonies" and "Still Life in Motion."

Wayne Bowman has had work published in The Exquisite Corpse, Eclectica, Images In Script and Stark

Raving Sanity and is active in the Zoetrope writer's workshop. He is the Chair of History, Political Science, Performing and Visual Arts at Ferrum College where he serves as Professor of Theatre. Bowman holds the MFA in Play Writing from the University of Virginia.

Terri Carrion was conceived in Venezuela and born in New York to a Galician mother and a Cuban Father. She has lived in Los Angeles and Miami and currently nests in Northern California among the redwoods. Terri Carrion is the assistant editor of Big Bridge an online magazine of poetry, art and everything else. Her own poetry and photography has appeared and disappeared in various publications.

Ira Cohen is the author of Poems from the Akashic Record and maker of the film Kings with Straw Mats. He is known around the world for his poems, his photographs, his films, and his recordings. He published the famous magazine Gnaoua in Morocco. His life is a magic carpet.

Josh Davis is a prolific writer and part-time rock god. He is working on his third novel "Under the Blue Banner of Heaven."

Willie Davis, a native of Whitesburg, Kentucky, has been referred to as "devilishly handsome" (Newsweek), "exhibiting Cary Grant style handsomeness punctuated by a boyish vulnerability" (Kirkus Reviews) and "so handsome I could cry" (Jonathan Yardley, Washington Post). He is widely acknowledged to be more handsome than Norman Mailer, Philip Roth and Joyce Carol Oates. He hopes to one day be more handsome than F Scott Fitzgerald.

Mikey Delgado didn't serve in the navy or attend university and is not drawn to Germanic folklore yet.

Bryan Edenfield probably doesn't exist but if he does his name is more likely Wayne. He was once fat but that was a long time ago and he has spent the better part of a burrito deconstructing his appetite. His most redeeming quality is he doesn't care.

Timothy Gager is the author of Short Street and Twenty-Six Pack, both collections of short fiction and the e-book, The Damned Middle::Life in a Drunken Slumber. His first book of poetry, The same corner of the Bar, is available through Ibbetson Street Press and his most recent, We Needed A Night Out, was released in 2006. He hosts the Dire Series in Cambridge, Massachusetts every month and is the co-founder of Somerville News Writers Festival. Timothy is the founding co-editor of The Heat City Literary Review and has edited the book, Out of the Blue Writers Unite: A Book of Poetry and Prose from the Out of the Blue Art Gallery. A graduate of the University of Delaware, Timothy lives in Waban, Massachusetts and is employed as a social worker.

Andy Henion's fiction has appeared or is forthcoming in Ink Pot, Pindeldyboz.com, Monkeybicycle.net, Thieves Jargon, Rumble, Plots with Guns, Old Crow Review, Lynx Eye, Gorilla, Poor Mojo's Almanac. He lives in the upper Midwest with some other people and a dog.

Ms. Jean Kang lives and "works" in New York City.

Adam P. Knave is the author of the Strange Angel series and Crazy Little Thing as well as numerous other fiction and non-fiction works scattered throughout the land. He lives in New York where he collects butter for nefarious purposes.

Stephen Moran is from Dublin originally and from London unoriginally. He would like to be a highly paid amateur and confound his creditors. Yes, confound them. He has one book of short stories out, "The London Silence." He also contributes to a number of websites, including his own www.stephenmoran.net.

Amy Muldoon lives an unterribly interesting life and secretly writes mass market paperback fiction for a living. She is currently working on a new novel, and a collection of short stories.

Zink Poe: Her writing is her road to recovery. Trust the pen.

Kenji Siratori (born in 1975) is a cult writer from Hokkaido in Japan. His short stories Tattoo and Hallucination=cell have appeared in 3A.M. Magazine. His novel Blood Electric is hailed in some quarters as a cyberpunk classic.

Dean Strom would never want to admit that anything we wrote about him is true. He was once observed nearly objectively using a new process called rebound-effect2 but there was 1 dissenter out of 107. Think how many that is out of 6,502,938,629, latest world population estimate 10:09 GMT (EST USA+5) Mar 12, 2006.

Dude Wallers has worked in a fish packing plant in Alaska, he has sold tropical fish next door to a biker bar in the inner city, managed exhibits at a public aquarium, and taught fishermen in the South Pacific how to keep them alive. Dude has worked in a nuke lab, sold wine in the Napa Valley and watched bugs mate. Dude holds a non-literary PhD. Dude's fiction has appeared at The Exquisite Corpse and Thieves Jargon.

Laszlo Xalieri, after having spent thirty-four of his thirty-six years in Georgia, has finally owned up to being a Southern writer. Pass the bourbon and bullets.